Breakfast with Scot

Also by Michael Downing

Fiction

A Narrow Time
Mother of God
Perfect Agreement

Drama

The Last Shaker

Breakfast
with
Scot

A NOVEL

Michael Downing

COUNTERPOINT
WASHINGTON, D.C.

Library of Congress Cataloging-in-Publication Data
Downing, Michael.
    Breakfast with Scot : a novel / Michael Downing.
        p.   cm.
    ISBN 1-58243-027-6 (alk. paper)
    I. Title.
PS3554.09346874   1999
813'.54—dc21   99-35584
                                                    CIP

FIRST PRINTING

Text design by Heather Hutchison

Printed in the United States of America on acid-free paper that
meets the American National Standards Institute Z39-48 Standard.

COUNTERPOINT
P.O. Box 65793
Washington, D.C. 20035-5793

Counterpoint is a member of the Perseus Books Group.

10 9 8 7 6 5 4 3 2 1

For Susanna

It is a great temptation to try to make the spirit explicit.

—*Wittgenstein*

Breakfast with Scot

one

At the end of his first week in Cambridge, I took Scot across
the river to the Isabella Stewart Gardner Museum. Scot was
eleven, and I figured he would feel at home in Boston's
famous bijou palace. It is jam-packed with Japanese screens,
French stained glass, German altars, Persian rugs, Italian
paintings, and no end of esteemed bric-a-brac. I didn't know
Scot well, but I knew he liked flea markets and jumble sales,
and I am astonished that I am about to tell you that I was
embarrassed by Scot's peculiarly limp limbs and his gooney
posture and I was hoping to stand him next to the pre-
Renaissance paintings and see his likeness in those charm-
ingly misproportioned saints and angels.

I wanted a new angle on Scot.

I wanted to lose perspective.

We were on the third floor, in the Gothic Room, when Scot
started to get sick to his stomach. Vertigo. He was okay if he
kept to the center of the shiny cobblestone floor, but he

1

couldn't stop himself from occasionally glancing through the Islamic arches into the empty air of the central courtyard. He asked the security guard how long a fall down it was to the ground-floor greenery, and when the guy said, "Let's take a look," and put a hand on his back, Scot's knees gave out, and as he collapsed, he squeaked out the words, "Please, stop it, sir."

The guard backed off, and he raised his hands to prove, I guess, that he wasn't a molester.

I waved at the guard, a no-harm-done gesture, and I said, "He's afraid of heights. It's not your fault."

But the guard was embarrassed and insulted, an emotional cocktail that Scot serves up to many strangers. He said, "What's the matter with that kid?" just loud enough to make it hurt. Then he wandered into the next room.

Scot said, "I'm sorry I screamed."

I pulled him to his feet. "You know those empty spaces I showed you on the walls downstairs? The paintings that were stolen?" It was true. Somebody had walked out of the place with a collection of Dutch masters worth millions. "Everybody's been in a bad mood around here since then."

We were only a few feet from my favorite painting in America, a small golden moment made by the Italian genius Giotto six hundred and seventy-five years ago. *The Presentation of the Infant Jesus in the Temple* is displayed on an easel—an inspired choice by Isabella, who acquired and placed everything in the museum while it was still her home. The Giotto is a genuine masterwork, and the easel makes you mindful of its humble origins. A man mixed up some egg-tempera paints and applied them to a small board. That's the history of art. The easel, unfortunately, is draped in red, a dash too much dash for me, but not for Scot.

Scot didn't comment on the flabby body of the baby Jesus. Held high on his back in Simeon's red-robed arms, Jesus steadies himself by clinging to Simeon's beard with his left hand as he reaches toward his mother's outstretched arms with his right, and his body becomes a casual crucifix. Something sad shadows this golden moment.

Scot was fascinated by the drapery. "You know, Ed, you could do that with your furniture at home," he said. "Or a bike."

Four young women arrived with big pads of paper, and they were followed by two handsome young men who'd obviously shopped for clothes in the novels of F. Scott Fitzgerald. One of them had found a pair of white bucks.

Scot instantly recognized the young men as a better version of Sam and me.

The guard came back, none too happy with any of the malingerers in the Gothic Room. He warned each one of the sketchers not to sit in the carved mahogany thrones, torture devices that no American would mistake for chairs.

Scot snapped open the blue leather camera bag slung over his shoulder.

The guard called out, "Sorry. No pictures in here, son." He looked at me accusingly.

Scot rummaged in his bag and finally fished out a vial of pink lotion. He jiggled a big blob into one palm, rubbed his hands together vigorously, packed and snapped things back into place, and stood up.

The lotion was fragrant beyond reason.

I heard the guard sniff.

I stared at Saint Simeon, the baby's hand in his beard.

One of the sketchers asked her friend if she smelled something funny.

The man with the bucks said, "That shouldn't be allowed," and pulled his linen friend to the next room. This was too outré for them. Draped furniture, yes. Stinky perfume, no.

The guard said, "That's some strong stuff."

Scot looked happy. To me, confidentially, he said, "It's called Pink Gardenia. It was on sale. I also bought the bath splash." Then he placed his slippery hand in mine, and we headed for the stairs.

two

Sam and I first met Scot when he was two and his hair was thin and pinkish, a condition optimistically referred to as strawberry blond. He spent most of that weekend under an oak table playing with everyone's shoelaces. I didn't think much about it at the time, but it is true that Scot treated every movable object as a hat. He tried on upholstered pillows, stray socks, notepads, and even a roasted chicken leg. His mother, Julie, had just moved in with Sam's only brother, Billy, who had a handsome old apartment in a Baltimore brownstone. Julie cooked too much food for every meal, which endeared her to me. She wanted Sam and me to have a false impression of her.

Billy is two years older than Sam, several inches shorter, and something happened to him at college that made him fall in love with Latin America. He'd always had dark hair and black eyes, but he was not always magnetic. He wears shabby dark suits, a thin dark tie, black boots, and spectacularly expensive white shirts. (This, he told me, was a tip from his Uncle Arthur, a quiet man who had a mustache Billy admired as a kid and a girlfriend who had always just dropped in when Sam and Billy happened to visit.) Billy also became a reader in college, and his fervor can transform any printed material into erotica. He often walks away from a dinner table midsentence and returns with his white sleeves jumbled up around his elbows, an open book balanced in his palm. He reads long passages and slaps himself on the head and groans as if the words are too fucking much and Jesus Christ Almighty can you believe this was just sitting on the shelf in my office and none of us knew a goddamned thing about it before this minute?

The second time Sam and I saw Scot, he was four. His hair was red, his eyes were gray, and he washed his toys after he played with them. Billy had spent the last eighteen months in Colombia. I'd sent Julie a few postcards and the name of a friend of mine who'd opened a gallery in D.C. Julie was a painter who hadn't had much luck. Billy told me how much it meant to him that I had called Julie every month and that I'd got her connected to so many art types. This further endeared Julie to me. She wanted Billy to have a false impression of me. Billy said he wanted to take us all out to dinner on the U.S. government, and Julie wore pearls. We all ordered exotic fish, and we drank Chilean wine, but after dinner the conversation turned hypothetical and tragic. Billy convinced us that he was important enough to be assassinated, and Julie looked proud when her fate got tangled up in his misfortunes and she ended up in an exploding car or blindfolded in a supply closet at the Miami airport. "Or it could be much more ignominious, " Billy said. "We could die in a plane crash."

Julie sounded a little drunk when she said, "Who are you kidding? We never go anywhere together."

Billy said, "I'm just saying there could be an accident."

Julie said, "You don't believe in accidents."

Billy said, "I'm just saying," and his black eyes gave us no hint of what he wasn't saying.

"Me, too," said Julie, who had taken off her pearl necklace and coiled it around Billy's hand.

Billy held his hand over Julie's plate, and the pearls ticked down around her picked-over fish.

Julie was impressed and a little amused and somehow she was even drunker. "The point is Billy dies in a plane crash, and I end up drinking myself to death. Right?"

Billy said, "Whatever it takes," very quietly, and filled Julie's glass, and the fun drained right out of the evening.

Sam poured himself more wine so Julie wouldn't have to die alone, but Julie ignored the gesture and yelled to the waiter, "Another bottle of a better red, something decent," and Billy nixed the order, and I said nobody is going to die, and Sam said nobody is going to die, and Billy said, "If we do die, we just want you to take care of Scot, that's all."

Julie said, "Just Scot, that's all. Just my son, that's all."

I said, "Well, of course, we love Scot," which was not true. We thought he was a sad kid, and we pitied him, but the whole evening had a spirit of exaggeration.

Sam said, "Are you sure?"

I thought he was talking to me, and Julie thought she was supposed to answer, so we said "Of course" at the same time, which saved me a moment's embarrassment and sealed Scot's fate.

The third time we saw Scot, he was almost seven and someone—Julie couldn't remember who—had sent him a feather boa, which Scot used as a wig. A beehive in the morning, a ponytail that afternoon. And Billy asked me if I thought Julie's paintings were any good. They were not. She was never trained, and she wasn't naive, so her attempts at abstraction were achingly artistic, and her figurative paintings were filled with unconvincing objects apologetically placed off-center. You could hear Julie saying, Let me get this tree out of your way, and just ignore those sort of bird things in the sky.

Billy poked at my silence. "Is she terrible? I mean, embarrassing?"

"I'm embarrassed about this conversation, Billy."

He said, "This is serious."

I said, "Then maybe you oughta talk to a serious art critic."

"But you don't think she's great."

I said I didn't think she was great.

I'd confirmed something for him. And years later, I wonder if I should have surprised him. Would Billy have loved Julie if I'd given him a false impression of her talent?

That weekend, when I woke on Sunday, Sam and Julie were making plans to cook breakfast. Scot had painted a pair of kneesocks on his legs. Billy and I went out to get the *Post* and the *Times* and to examine a photograph of a still life by Julie. Billy had pulled into a half-full church parking lot. He put the picture on the dashboard and said, "How much could you get for this? Tops."

I asked him how big the original was. I hoped it was small. It was a genuine clunker. On a golden background, Julie had drawn an apple and an orange. The apple was painted orange, and the orange was splotchy red and green, somewhat like an apple.

"Julie sold this the last time I was away. She always makes a couple of big sales when I'm away. She's been using again.

Unless you tell me this is worth four thousand dollars, I'm taking that posting in Santiago. I'm not the kid's father, and I'm not funding any more of this arts and crafts shit. And I gotta get a blood test. Me. And wouldn't that be ironic?"

"What?" I was thinking about art. Scot's painted knee-socks, for instance.

Billy said, "Ironic if it's me instead of Sam who ends up with AIDS." He got out of the car. "You wanna come in and say a prayer for me before the blood test? I'm not staying for the whole deal or anything."

I waited in the car with the photograph of Julie's painting. Apples and oranges. Get it?

Julie and Billy. They shared a sense of irony.

three

Billy took the job, Julie took the apartment, and Scot took a powder.

Sam spoke to Billy a few times a year, and they always made complicated travel plans, which they treated like piñatas, smashing them to bits with scheduling problems, ticket prices, disappointing weather predictions, and work, work, work. I don't know what Billy got out of it, but Sam usually salvaged the name of a casino in Barbados or a volcanic lake in Guatemala, and I'd buy a map and order up some brochures, and we'd bring them to the Cape in August and tell our friends that they shouldn't count on us renting the house with them next summer.

Julie remained in my postcard rotation right up until the end, so it would be untrue to say that I never gave a thought to her or Scot. The last time I spoke to her was in June, when my friend Nula and I were telling everyone we knew that Marco, the industrialist who owned *Figura*, our employer, was laying out 85,000 American dollars for roses to brighten

up the Gardner Museum, which he'd reserved for an autumn party to mark the first anniversary of the English-language edition of *Figura*, Europe's most something magazine. Most expensive? Most superfluous? Most unlikely to survive its first year in America? Nula and I were supposed to fill in the blank on the invitations.

Julie's last call came very early on a sunny Saturday morning, and she told me she'd been in town for a while. I invited her to come stay at Finn Street, and she hesitated, so I scaled back the invitation to dinner, thinking I'd overestimated the remains of what little we had shared. The dinner invitation really confused her, and before I could suggest a coffee in the Square, Julie started to cry. She wasn't in Boston. She was in New York, or at least it looked like New York from where she was sitting. I told her I could send her money, and she said, "I'm not messed up. I just wanted to talk to Billy." I offered to get Sam, and Julie sounded sober when she said, "Never mind. I don't want to talk to Billy while I'm messed up." I asked if Scot was with her, and Julie said, "Didn't he go to my mother's for the summer?" She sounded genuinely curious, as if she and Scot had been classmates in grade school. A lot of people pass through our lives. We can't keep track of them all. I asked Julie if there was anything I could do for her. Lightly, reassuringly, Julie said, "Oh, no. But I'll tell Scot you were asking for him. And thanks a lot for calling, Sam."

Sam tried and failed to rouse Billy in Santiago to find out if Julie had a mother. Billy hadn't surfaced since December, when he'd called from a hotel in the Peruvian Andes and announced that he might be getting married to a woman from Charlottesville. She and her six-year-old kid were living with him. Billy always had a soft spot for fatherless families, and Sam counted it as an embarrassing flaw, as if Billy was some kind of predator. Billy's temporary adoptive urges were not psychological, or not simply so. Growing up, he had a regular family. Sam and Billy's parents stuck around until they died, and even in their old age they always had a lot of ham salad and olives on hand in case their kids showed up with friends.

Nula had a new theory about Billy, and she was entitled. She'd been subjected to fifteen years of Billy stories. Lately, she was off him. She'd bought his line to Sam about coming north for Thanksgiving that year, and she was still acting jilted. One Sunday morning, Nula dropped by to announce that Billy was a romantic entrepreneur, someone who anticipated trends, "like early investors in McDonald's. Single mothers are a growing franchise." Nula explained, "There's always somebody advertising for part-time help or a night manager who may or may not turn out to be partner material."

I thought Billy saw himself as an outlaw, and he only entered homes with well-marked exits.

He eventually called in early September—a Monday morning, when he wouldn't have to talk to Sam, since even Billy knew that was Sam's busiest day. Sam's a chiropractor, and the weekends leave a lot of people bent over and achy. Billy had an old address for Julie's mother in Troy, New York, and he said he was relieved to know Julie wasn't dead, which, by then, she was.

four

Sam stopped shaving on the last Friday of August, the day Julie died. Helen, Julie's sister, called from Troy and told us there wasn't going to be a service right away, but she'd spoken to a lawyer and a social worker and her mother in a nearby nursing home, and Scot was going back to camp while we readied his room. Sam said, "If they could, they'd fax him to us. Poor kid." Poor kid, indeed. I was one half of the welcoming committee, and I spent most of that weekend canvassing our friends and neighbors, soliciting their petty prejudices and moral outrage. Unfortunately, everyone was relentlessly encouraging, and those who had children of their own were gleeful. Joan Koester up the street spoke for the fruitful when she said, "Welcome to our world. Hope you didn't have any plans to see a movie or to eat in a real restaurant for the next eight years. You and Sam are screwed. For me and Greg, though, this will be delightful. We get to feel progressive, and because we are petty, we'll enjoy getting even with you guys."

13

Sam was undaunted. And I probably should have been inspired by his uncomplaining sense of duty. It was maddening. He spent Sunday scheduling double sessions with his patients, to buy himself extra vacation days. But it was his beard, which was growing in gray and black, that kept me at bay. Sam had trimmed it already. He was going to have one of those short, neat beards. He looked suddenly older and—I hated to have to say it to myself—nattier. Sam was turning into a dapper middle-aged man.

He left the house at six on Monday morning.

I slept until seven—well, it was eight. He'd left me a charmless note on the kitchen table: Meeting with Barbara at six (attorney). I read the note several times, and then it was eight-thirty. Nula was at the corner of Garden Street and Appian Way, lighting a cigarette. She'd only smoke half: even her beloved cigarettes let her down. I was still thinking about making coffee. Before she gave up on me and walked to the office alone, Nula would check her Swiss Army watch one last time. She admired the Swiss for charging too much for everything, as did Marco, owner and publisher of *Figura*, the monthly magazine of monumental art that was published almost every month by a staff of seventy Italians and three and a half Americans, unevenly divided between Milan and Cambridge. Marco liked to scare the American staff by threatening to move the English operations to Geneva. He answered every proposal for an article on Native American art with this word. "Geneva. Do the Swiss complain that there is no yodeling at La Scala? No. They buy orchestra seats and starch their shirts and push past the Americans waiting in a queue for last-minute discount seats in the thirteenth balcony. Am I speaking a clear English? I don't want to hear about your totem poles or those burial mounds in your middle lands. In Geneva, they have a world-famous lake," he said, "and they happily waste a week's salary on a handbag. I will prosper there."

"He's right," Nula had said after Marco apologized and promised to fire a few of the Italians and replace the folding chairs in the American editorial offices with something from the industrial design catalog he left with Nula. "He oughta open an office in the Alps," she explained. "Only a Nazi would want one of these."

Nula would not want me to want Scot.

I was an hour late, which in Nula time was an hour and a half, since she'd started counting the moment she left her house. She was seated at one end of the two white folding tables we'd pushed together to make a decent desk in the attic of the colonial mansion Marco refused to furnish or air-condition. She was wearing a gigantic yellow silk shirt. Nula was short and slim, and if most days she appeared to have borrowed her father's clothes, then her father appeared to be Louis XIV.

I said, "I think I might have to leave Sam."

Nula was working her way furiously through two piles of paper, shuffling them into a sequenced stack. "Look at what the fax dragged in," she said.

It was the dreaded page proofs of the Dome Project, an article by one of Marco's Italian mistresses. As I unfolded one of the stacked black metal chairs, Nula handed me a back issue of the magazine.

"Sam told me we have to start using cushions," she explained. "These chairs are screwing with our spines."

Sam serviced many of our friends. And he touched more than their backs. He touched their lives. There were still days when this intimacy seemed to accrue as an advantage to him.

Sam's chiropractic was not classical, though he was a master of the momentary manipulations and sudden adjustments that restored a body's alignment and repaired cranky neural circuits. Most people who sought out Sam had bum backs and insurance companies that balked at his fees, though they liked to reimburse surgeons for chopping out a few vertebrae or severing some nerves before the policyholder limped over to Cambridge without a referral.

There were two kinds of chiropractors: straight and not straight. I am not making this stuff up. It was not redundant to say that Sam was not a straight chiropractor who was not straight. Some of the straight-schoolers liked to be called "superstraight," and I thought of them as the Aryans of Adjustment. They opposed fluoride in the water supply, and they thought the germ theory of disease was propaganda perpetrated by your local pharmacist. The straights were outnumbered by broad-scope practitioners, the blenders and mixers. Sam had attended a straight training college, but he had a Ph.D. in biology, added bleach to his laundry, regularly ordered up MRIs and CAT scans to supplement his in-office X rays, and he shopped for tea in Chinatown. In chiropractic terms, Sam was a fancy high-speed blender with many attachments.

But his practice had another dimension. He talked about the sources of pain in people's lives, and Jeremy, his longtime partner, cautioned Sam about his "excessive interest in the patient histories," which was one way of saying Jeremy saw 135 patients per week and Sam hadn't cracked a hundred. Jeremy wanted Sam to behave like a real doctor, and he bought them matching lab coats and eventually found them space in a handsome brick building teeming with fully reimbursable optometrists and podiatrists. It was a beauty of a building in Harvard Square, the old reversible shirt collar factory, and after Sam paid the contractors to build him a display case and dispensary for his collection of remedial and restorative teas, which he and his devotees drank, inhaled, and mixed into their bathwater, Jeremy went to work for an HMO. Sam stopped eating red meat, white sugar, and snacks in bags, and for a while I worried that the Clorox was next.

But, as Nula said, there was nothing to worry about as long as Sam was still willing to eat a roasted chicken. The tea thing, she assured me, was not homeopathic. It was homey. She washed her hair in a Sam chamomile special, and she and Sam both urged me to take an occasional soak in ginger root and lemons to improve my skin, which was flaky. And after stewing in the muddy waters of managed care for a year and a half, Jeremy bought his way back into Sam's practice, and he didn't bring along his lab coat.

I liked Jeremy. He was as insecure as I was, and twice as impulsive, so he often saved me the trouble of offending Sam myself.

But Scot? I didn't see him as value-added to the partnership.

Nula zipped across the room and ducked into the eaves, returned with several manila folders, and cracked open a black marker with her teeth. Logged, sorted, and labeled: the Dome Project was neatly laid out. "We'll deal with that cadaver later," she said. Then she dipped into her red folder, her collection of odd jobs and annoyingly tiny tasks. She pulled out a page of typeset captions stapled to the hand-scribbled originals, traded the black pen for a green, transposed a few letters and corrected the punctuation. In seconds, it was initialed, dated, tucked into the To Be Faxed folder, and Nula needed a break.

She opened one side of the nearest casement window, and stuck her hennaed head out into Cambridge's best neighborhood.

Nula's work habits were epileptic. A fit of productivity and then blotto.

At the other end of the large, white room, Eleanor Covena's blue computer screen was shining, but the managing editor's chair was leaning against the wall behind her table. Theo, the half-time fact-checker, was also just a collapsed chair and a computer screen this morning.

"Eleanor called." Nula was back. "She claims she's sick, but she never gets sick."

We both suspected that Eleanor Covena was not long for the world of monumental art. Eleanor still referred to the way things were done at the *Atlantic*, a monthly magazine that actually appeared monthly. And the last time Marco turned up, Eleanor had presented him with a four-page request and justification for hiring an editorial assistant.

Marco pretended to read the documentation. He was wearing a double-breasted blueberry wool suit, and he'd spent the morning having his hair frosted. "You seem to be accusing me of fraud," he said jovially, as if people often did.

Either she was too tall or Marco was too short, but Eleanor looked like a bully when she snatched the pages from him. She tried to sound contrite when she said, "Fraud? I just need a secretary, Marco."

Marco tucked the ends of his olive green scarf under his crisp lapels. He looked like a prince and a pigeon. "Don't be ridiculous, Eleanor. You are the head editor for America. You need an executive assistant, but you cannot afford one. For now, fax me whatever you need, and I will personally have someone in Milan do it for you."

Nula said, "Face it, Ed. You can't leave Sam." She was sitting on the floor, probably doing yoga.

I was printing out the email sent the night before from Milan. We Americans were perpetually behind our colleagues, a day late. It made us feel Italian.

Nula climbed back into her chair. "I love you too much, pal o' mine, and if you left Sam, I'd have to stop seeing him professionally. And I am too selfish to give up my adjustments, so I'd have to lie to you and sneak off and strip for Sam. We'd all be stuck in a loveless massage à trois. No thanks."

"But the kid?"

Nula sprang to her feet and slapped her hands on the table. She leaned into me like a preacher. "Fuck that Billy. If he'd come to Cambridge ten years ago, we'd all be happy now. This kid is trouble. You don't know squat about him. He could be another one of those bald kids—"

"The Burlingtons."

"One more bald kid on Finn Street and you might as well call 911 because somebody's house is about to be torched. And which bedroom does he get? The nice one next to yours or that mean little casket where you keep the treadmill?"

"StairMaster," I said. Nula was right. This kid was a threat to our health.

"Besides the fact that you were a kid once, do you know anything about ten-year-old boys that might qualify as useful?"

I said, "I'm pretty sure he's eleven."

"Eleven?" Nula made it sound like a felony. "Eleven is much worse than ten. I gotta smoke again."

I picked up the nearest of several espresso cups and emptied out the rubber bands. "Nobody's coming in today," I said, "Here's an ashtray."

Nula lit up.

For a minute there, we were happy. One of our great shared pleasures was the misappropriation of household objects. Ballpoint-pen coffee stirrers. Wastebasket footstools. Postcard dustpans. Magazine seat cushions.

Nula dealt out two piles of the Dome Project. "Let's save all that email for lunch, okay?" She was agitated and ready to work.

I fished two pairs of eyeglasses from the jam jar of pens— half lenses, black plastic frames, plucked from a drugstore carousel. Without magnification, every page of *Figura* was an optical illusion. The articles and captions were reverse printed in an ancient and elaborate and illegible typeface, and the white letters swam in a sea of a different color every month. The Dome Project was slated for March, and the pages were reddish.

Nula muttered, "There's something weird about this red."

"Tomato soup," I said.

Nula ditched her cigarette and pressed the butt end of a pen to her forehead. "It's a mail-order migraine," she said.

And after work, after leaving Nula at our corner and heading for my collision with Sam and his attorney, I understood something. I hadn't become a sculptor or a painter. Every year I took some pictures of a maple tree in the Berkshires, and that was my career as a photographer. I'd dropped out of the Buddies program after my guy moved into a hospice to die. I'd lived in a house for seven years without knocking down a single wall, and I hadn't added a skylight or a spare bathroom. I owed my sister several letters and a phone call, and she had four kids and a contract for the third mystery in her *Diana in Danger* series for young readers. Sam paid two-thirds of the mortgage, and he worked late a few nights every month at Cambridge City Hospital, adjusting old veterans for free. I never wanted a kid. Sam never wanted a kid. We were getting a kid because Sam believed a man is meant to make good on his word, and because I hadn't seeded and watered and weeded my garden, and now, when I needed it, I had no abundant supply of garlic to ward off the little vampire.

Sam's lawyer, Barbara, worked on the second floor of a converted gambrel roof home in mid-Cambridge. She led Sam and me into her conference room, which had once been two bedrooms. She was wearing a black linen dress, yellow rubber gardening clogs, a few paper clips in her hair, and you just didn't ask. When she had to represent you in a public courtroom, Barbara sent Althea, a stern Haitian woman with real shoes who didn't wear the office supplies.

Barbara sat opposite us, and we were all blinded by the sun, which sparked and shimmered on the surface of the black-lacquer dining table until she groped her way to the bay window and tilted the slats of the blinds. "Fundamentally, there are three recognized forms of guardianship," she said. According to Sam, Barbara talked like a normal person when they were alone, but whenever I was along she spoke slowly and often referred to her notes, as if I had a countersuit pending. It was no secret that she didn't like me. I was almost forty, and I wasn't important enough to retain an attorney of my own, and her partner, Donna, was once married to a college classmate of mine. It didn't matter that I didn't know the guy. It was a small art school in Rhode Island, and Barbara figured I was lying.

Barbara coughed, to alert us to the importance of what she was about to say. "Without the participation of an extrarelational female, the male homosexual partnership cannot be expected to yield a person whom the State would designate as a natural guardian, or guardian by nature."

Whatever humor Barbara had, she'd spent it on her shoes. It's too bad, because she was a font of fascinating information. Guardianship, for instance. A biological parent is a guardian by nature, a status Sam and I could not achieve as a couple. I didn't mind. Unlike many of my contemporaries, I'm comforted whenever the State takes its lead from Nature. I've seen plenty of boy dogs humping, but I've never seen a pregnant one. I rely on the precedent, so why shouldn't my elected leaders?

You can also become a guardian by judicial appointment, but if you are like Sam and me, well, it's not very likely. Here, I'd say the State strays from the ways of Nature. Scrawny male moose orphans butt heads with same-sex elders. In fact, almost all solitary animals who have been weaned prefer the rough-and-tumble of an indiscriminate herd or a motley pack to the confines of a kennel or the pound. If you don't believe me, just open the cage. And yet the State persists in putting kids in the can instead of homes occupied by the likes of us.

The third way is testamentary. This was our case, and Barbara became especially tendentious. "In this case," she said, reading directly from her lecture notes, "the burden falls to the State to deliver the ward and his or her property expeditiously to the person identified as guardian of recourse in the final will and testament of the natural parent."

"And Julie named us," said Sam, trying to speed things along.

Too late. Barbara had pulled an orange from somewhere beneath the table. "Diabetes," she said, and I didn't believe her. If she'd found a chocolate bar under there, she wouldn't have offered it around either. "Julie named you, Sam. Ed is entirely beside the point."

Because I had no comeback, I eyed the big binder clip on a stack of papers, and I almost put it in my hair.

Barbara slid a photocopy of Julie's will into Sam's hands. "No one is disputing the will or its terms. It's official." She paused. "But I have two additional letters here that bother me." She pulled them out of an Express Mail envelope and flattened the folds so Sam could read them. "At first, I was bothered by the fact of their existence. This is overkill. The will itself establishes guardianship. Why did Julie go to these additional lengths? This one appears to have been written by Julie, confirming a conversation with you about the guardianship. Your brother, Billy, is the signatory witness."

Sam nodded and glanced at his watch.

"And this one, allegedly written by you, bears a signature that looks remarkably like your brother's. And oddly unlike your own."

Sam nodded.

I could read the letter from Sam that Sam hadn't written or signed. It was dated at least a year before our dinner with Julie and Billy and the Chilean wine.

Sam said, "Did Julie's lawyer send these?"

Barbara ate the last two segments of her orange before she said yes. "He thought they'd have some sentimental value for you, or for the ward later on in life. These are the originals, but I'll have them copied for you before you leave."

Sam nodded, and he looked at me, as if to say, now do you see how she earns her retainer?

I hadn't understood a thing since the orange appeared.

Sam said, "You want to say something else about the letters."

"I want to say they are superfluous," Barbara said. "They have no legal merit. But they do have a demerit. I've read them, and I am fairly certain that one person wrote both of them. My best guess is Billy." She pointed out the forgery of Sam's signature again. "But why?"

Sam snagged the two letters. "These mean nothing now. For the record, you never read them, Barbara. You waited to open the envelope in my presence, so I could read them first. You left the room. Something you had to ask your secretary. I accidentally took the letters home with so many other papers, and I filed them away. We never mentioned them again."

Barbara shut her eyes as though her blood sugar had dropped. "Better to be thorough now than indicted later." She left the room, spoke to her secretary, and joined us again. "Should I be nervous now, Sam?"

"No." Sam slipped the letters into the Express Mail envelope. "Leaving the room was overkill, really, but a nice touch. I'm sentimental. That's my crime."

I'd never seen an actual backroom deal, and I was impressed. But Sam wasn't done. As he slipped the letters into his briefcase, he said, "Call the sister in Troy and tell her to have Scot at her house and packed by noon next Tuesday. The fifth graders go to school next week. He ought to start with everyone else. We have Labor Day to get things ready for him. How could they send him back to camp on his own?"

Barbara said, "There will be a social worker present, in Troy. Until you arrive, he's technically a ward of the state."

Sam stood up and said, "Just two more things. I never want Scot to hear anyone refer to him as a ward of any kind. And Ed is never beside the point. Ed is the point. I begin and end with Ed."

Sam's beard, I noticed, wasn't natty anymore. It was cool. And his arm around my shoulder—also cool.

five

Sam and I spent the Labor Day weekend doing every useless thing we could think of short of boiling water. I mowed the lawn. He washed windows. I bought new sheets and towels while he acquired a month's supply of breakfast cereal in little boxes. Mildred Monterosso dragged over a collection of tools and pails and an old tire with a rope, which took us a while to understand as a swing. Joan and Greg strolled by several times with four-year-old Hank and laughed at us, and later in the day Greg attached the tire to the limb of a sturdy old apple tree. Robert and Danny drove over from Boston without their feral poodle and helped us move furniture around. On Sunday, Nula arrived with brioche for Sam, a genuine coffee from the Heyday for me, and a spectacular assortment of personal bathroom supplies for Scot, which she'd packed inside an old wooden box with a working skeleton key. She'd written a welcome note on a postcard of Cambridge, but she'd spelled his name wrong. "Scot with one *t?*

That's the one other thing I'll do for that kid. Before I die, he's gonna have another *t*."

And Monday was another buffet of friends and neighbors and plausible toys and implausible winter boots. Andrea Burlington and her boys watched from their windows across the street, and occasionally the boys' new father would wander out to smoke and inspect our piles. Our houses were twins—white shingled workers' cottages built at the turn of the century—and we shared the dead end of Finn Street the way kids share a double bed. We monitored the border.

Joan and Greg Koester stayed away on Monday. They decided to clean out the empty side of their big, yellow duplex at the corner, and they called often to brag about how messy their place was compared to ours. They lived on the quiet Finn Street side and rented out the trafficky Massachusetts Avenue half of their house. Their opposites, the dashing young marrieds who'd bought the other corner house, a blue Victorian folly, didn't speak to the rest of us except to inquire about the provenance of used condoms and garbage lids they found among their geometric shrubs. No one could remember their names because Joan always called them the Lost Lovelies. It was clear they thought they'd bought a house in Harvard Yard. And you could walk there from Finn Street in ten minutes, but our only official connection to the University was the visiting professor at the law school, Joan and Greg's tenant-to-be, who was due in October. Between the Lost Lovelies and the Burlingtons was a small, sloping gray Greek revival with a pillared front porch we all coveted. Louisa Bamford had moved down to North Carolina, to "die in a hurricane," she said. Louisa had lived in the gray house since she was a child, and what she didn't know about the last eighty years on Finn Street she'd made up, always bothering to invent something intriguing or distinguished about the former residents of our homes. Her family was supposed to straighten up the saggy house and sell it, but the only improvement to date was the blossoming of a fall clematis that Louisa had looped around her fence before she left.

Mildred Monterosso lived in the aluminized ranch next door to us with her husband, George, and their middle-aged son, also George. They were kind, giant people who partially blocked our view of Joan and Greg, and on Monday afternoon all three Monterossos sat in our living room and ate the sandwiches Mildred had prepared. Before they left, the Georges, who were masons, inspected our basement and promised to do something about "the worst of it," and Mildred said, "Don't mind them. Your basement's been here longer than they have. Those boys would caulk up the seams in my shoes if I didn't keep an eye on them." Then Jeremy, Sam's partner in back-cracking, showed up with balloons, and Barbara turned up in her yellow clogs carrying two teddy bears—one for Scot and one for me, I supposed—and someone from Milan called to say something Sam couldn't understand, and my sister must have paid a fortune to have three blue-and-white checked cereal bowls and three matching mugs delivered to our doorstep on a holiday.

Sam surprised me Tuesday morning when he said he wanted to drive to Troy by himself. "I don't want to foster any connection to people who didn't give his mother a proper burial and then packed him back off to camp. I won't do the rest of it alone. I promise." And when Scot walked into our house ahead of Sam at seven that evening, he was wearing slippered brown pajamas and Sam's V-neck sweater, and he glanced at the staircase, said "Hello, Ed," and ran up to his bedroom, the little one with the new sheets, and he didn't speak to me again until Wednesday morning, when he said, "I guess I'll see you tonight."

Scot arrived with almost nothing a boy might be expected to want or own. His clothes were unwashed and, for instance, neither of his bags contained a sweatshirt or a decent winter jacket. Sam looked confused. "You know, Julie's sister seemed like a decent woman. Helen. She was gracious, and she said I should let them know if they should write or call. It was only the second or third time Helen had met Scot. She's got three kids, I guess. I mean, I didn't meet them. They were at day care and nursery school, but I bet they have sweaters. She didn't even do his laundry."

I said, "I can do his laundry. We can take him shopping."

"I met Julie's mother. She wears a black pageboy wig. She asked me if I was going sailing." Sam looked at me for confirmation of something.

"Is she loopy?"

Sam said, "Dying of wine and cordials." He followed me to the kitchen and pulled a leg off the store-roasted chicken. "And it wasn't an overdose, just for the record. I got a copy of the coroner's report. Somebody—maybe Julie, maybe a dear friend—shot a needle full of air into her arm and killed her. And according to Helen, Scot thinks she was killed in a car accident. Can we go to bed soon?"

Sam ate a second chicken leg and went up to check on Scot. I stayed downstairs and checked out Scot's other bag, the bag of tricks. It was a black nylon duffel bag. I zipped it open and a pink hairbrush fell out and started to play a jangly lullaby, and I had to carry it to the kitchen and let the song expire. Next, I withdrew two plastic food containers filled with plastic beads and fake-gold chains. In a glass jam

jar, I found two pairs of white kneesocks, one with lacy
foldovers at the top. This gave me the willies. I felt I was holding a jar with a miniature Scot in formaldehyde, kneesocks
painted on his legs. I zippered the case and carried it up to
his room. Sam was asleep, sitting on the floor with his head
against the closet door. Scot had scooted down into his lap,
where he lay like an apostrophe.

On Wednesday morning, Scot refused to wear any socks,
and Sam walked him to his new school, which is on my way
to work, but I was afraid I'd ask a provocative sock question,
and by 11:30 Sam and Scot were at home together because
Scot refused to speak at school once Sam left. Scot seemed to
like the swing in the yard, and Sam called his office to cancel
all his regular appointments for the afternoon; and in less
than twenty minutes, according to Sam, Tony Burlington,
one of the bald boys who lived directly across the street, was
threatening to kill Scot with one of those red iron steering-
wheel locks, and Sam had to hold Tony by the collar and
threaten him with the club until his mother came to the
window of their downstairs bathroom. Andrea Burlington
was sporting a surgical mask, as she did whenever there was
air in the air. She somehow made it clear that Tony had
skipped the first day of school, so Sam had to hold him until
the Cambridge police came and took him to homeroom.
Andrea Burlington and her kids got their money's worth out
of our tax dollars.

When I came home, Scot was walking up Mass. Ave. from
Harvard Square with Ryan, the other bald Burlington boy.
Ryan was two years older than Tony. I later discovered they
had been to Carnduff's, a venerable old pharmacy, which
specializes in Medicaid prescriptions and bath splash. Scot
stuffed a bag of something right into his tiny trousers, and

before I could ask any questions, Ryan split, and Scot told me about Tony's attempt on his life, and he was crying by the time we got into the house. Sam refused to display the red club he'd confiscated from Tony in our living room window, which Scot believed was his only chance to avoid getting beat up by Tony, who would surely want his weapon back. Sam slept with Scot again.

Thursday was complicated and disheartening and a little scary, too, and Sam and I knew we were speeding down a dark road in a borrowed car with no brakes. Scot begged Sam to let him wear one of our biking helmets to school in case Tony Burlington showed up, but he had to settle for an extra container of sugar-free chocolate pudding, which Sam said he could trade for his safety. Scot made it through the school day, and I met him at the front entrance, where he was sitting with his jersey pulled up over his head next to a fat Asian boy with braces, who introduced himself as the safety guard. He had a badge, and he apologized for not wearing it, but he was still waiting for the orange chest bands to be issued.

"Scot is scared to walk home, and he won't get in my mom's car. My name is Joey Morita, and I wouldn't mind being his friend someday." Joey pointed to the street, and his mother waved at us.

I walked Joey to the car with Scot, who was still hooded.

Mrs. Morita said, "Is he a boy or a girl?" I think she meant it teasingly, figuring it would elicit a manly display of gender identification.

Scot said, "I'm dropping out as soon as I can."

Mrs. Morita was staring at Scot, and it was harder and harder for her to smile, and she drove off without a word.

Before Scot dropped his guard, I got a good look at the belt he was wearing. It was shiny white imitation patent leather with pink dancing dogs and jazzy little musical notes.

That night Sam finally came to our bed, and he kissed my back, and I stiffened, and he said, "This is bad."

I said, "What's bad?" I stared at our clock.

"You're embarrassed."

"Yes, I am," I said.

"I am, too." Sam rested his hand on my hip. "But it's not exactly because he's in the house, is it?"

"Not exactly."

"What then?" Sam traced a crooked line down my thigh.

"Sometimes—too often, really—when I look at Scot, I see just what Tony Burlington sees."

Sam said, "But we're not the Burlington boys."

"That's right," I said, "and even the Burlington boys can see that."

Sam backed off.

six

Sam wanted to discuss the forged letters, and we'd reserved time with each other on Saturday night, but by then I'd been to the Gardner with Scot, and we'd eaten our Chinese food cold because Scot had heard Nula was coming on Sunday morning and, in a fit of gratitude for the hygiene kit, he'd decorated the front door with plastic appliqué tea roses, and Sam couldn't get them off with a steak knife or a paint scraper, and "Nobody understands me. Nobody understands me. Nobody understands."

And I know kids say so all the time, but I wonder if the words were ever truer spoken.

seven

Sunday morning was weirdly warm and still, and Sam was asleep when I rolled out of bed. I found the newspapers on the kitchen table, and I waited to grind my beans because I figured the noise would interrupt Scot and Ryan Burlington, whose conversation was drifting my way from the front stoop.

Scot wasn't entirely satisfied when Ryan explained that his brother Tony was just going though a violent phase. He pressed for protection from future attacks, and Ryan said, "Chill out. I told you, I took care of him," and Scot said, "I feel like kissing you for that," and Ryan said, "Well, don't. I ain't that high. But I wanna hear more about what your mother said about needles."

Scot said, "Let's face it, there's two kinds of needles. The clean kind delivers the real shit and the dirty kind is just dog shit. Usually, you can find a van and trade in your old ones for clean ones. Call the health department to check." His inflection didn't change when he said, "Can I touch your

34

head?" He must have copped a feel, because he giggled and then he sobered up and said, "I don't really like to think about scalps, but thanks, Ryan."

"Sure," said Ryan. "I should get goin' soon."

Ryan Burlington wasn't always such a sweet kid. When Sam and I first moved to the neighborhood, he and his brother rode their banana bikes in circles on the street outside our kitchen window and popped wheelies whenever they yelled "Faggots!" until their previous father dragged them away. But then Ryan got to high school, where he got high most days, and he acquired a harem of little Louise Brooks look-alikes, and his allegiance started to drift across the street, not exactly toward Sam and me, but away from his masked mother and his solemn new father.

Scot kept Ryan around a little longer with a pretty good explanation of how a desperate junkie can clean out his works in diluted bleach and, before he left, I think Ryan might have slipped Scot a dollar or two. Someone was funding Scot on the sly. Someone was keeping him in perfume and bath beads.

Scot joined me in the kitchen.

I said, "Thanks for bringing in the papers."

He said, "Really?"

I said, "Really."

"You're welcome, Ed," he said. He was wearing his brown pajamas and one of Sam's sweaters. He climbed up onto the counter and grabbed a checkered mug and bowl, and then he offered me a mug.

I said, "Really?"

He laughed and said, "Really."

I made the coffee. Scot chose a sweet cereal. We both paged through the paper. I poured us each a glass of orange juice. I offered to make toast, and Scot politely declined, but he did want to know if Sam and I were married.

I said we weren't.

Scot said, "That's what I thought."

And I thought, here we go.

Scot said, "You're just gay, right?"

I said, "And we love each other."

Scot said, "A lot of kids say I'm gay."

"What do you think they mean?" I was thinking Sam should've briefed me on house policy. I knew a few of the rules: Scot had to talk in school, he was not supposed to put on any perfume without permission, and he was no longer allowed to call our next-door neighbors Mr. and Mrs. Montasaurus.

Scot was studying a picture in the Sunday magazine. He put his spoon to his forehead. "I think they mean they don't really like any of us."

"Maybe," I said. "Or maybe they mean they don't know any of us yet." I knew it was lame, but it sounded vaguely optimistic and thus parental. Shamelessly, I sought refuge in the wisdom of the neighborhood philosopher. "What does Ryan Burlington say about it?"

Scot perked up. "Ryan says, love the one you're with."

I should have said something, but I was surprised. Ryan had done his homework.

Sam drifted down in his bathrobe and beard, and he liked what he saw. We looked benign, Scot and I and our matching mugs, but we were several eggs short of a healthy breakfast.

Sam's plans for the day were ambitious, and when he opted for minted green tea instead of coffee I knew he had not slept very well. Nula was dropping by at ten, and then we were going to shop for clothes, and he had to stop by his office, and somehow the three of us were supposed to spend our spare time making lists of questions and problems that we would discuss during dinner, besides which there were some house rules to clarify, including a ban on stickers and lighting matches indoors, and Scot had to take a bath and brush his teeth and clean up his room, and it was probably going to rain, so we had to shut the windows before we left, and thank god the kettle finally came to a boil.

Scot cupped his hand, blew into it, and sniffed. "I hope Ryan didn't notice my bad breath." He folded the corner of his page and closed the magazine.

Sam said, "And we're going to set some goals for the week. Like making at least one new friend."

Scot said, "Everybody?"

I looked to Sam for the answer, but he was warming one of his fancier clay teapots with hot-water rinses, and that meant he was more than tired. He said, "Everybody will have different goals."

My goal was sausage for breakfast, which was a non-starter, I could tell. Sam was heating up a bit of old kasha in nonfat milk with a dram of buckwheat honey. Whenever things went wrong, Sam got serious about food and ate mostly detergents like celery and egg whites and mean little grains that took more than they gave.

Scot said, "I'm sorry about the stickers, Sam."

Sam said, "Apology accepted," which seemed chary to me, but Scot looked relieved, and he went upstairs to deal with his messy desk and his bad breath.

I made toast.

Sam inhaled the tea fumes and finally drank some.

I drank more coffee.

Sam said, "We've got to be more mindful."

I said, "I've gotta get some new ties."

Sam said, "I don't want him hanging out with high-school kids."

"Sorry," I said.

Sam said, "Apology accepted." His breakfast was bubbling behind him. He didn't smile when he added, "It was a joke, Ed. Lighten up."

I said, "He wanted to know if we are married."

Sam said, "Scot raises a lot of questions." He stood up to save his breakfast from burning, but before he turned away he reached across the table and put the Sunday magazine on my plate.

I opened to the page Scot had marked. It was an ad. A handsome young man in a classic blue blazer. Starched white shirt. Enviable yellow paisley tie. Marble forehead and chin. Black hair. Blue eyes. Pale pink lipstick.

Eating the kasha calmed Sam. He was at ease, leaning back against the sink, his checkered bowl in his hand. "Scot has two makeup kits. Both of them pretty well used."

I said, "I don't suppose you found any cleats or a football in that bag of his?"

Sam said, "No, but there is a charm bracelet."

I said, "So, on the basis of the evidence, we can assume we're raising a drag queen."

Sam said, "We can assume he's not a halfback."

I said, "And a drag queen is to a halfback as—"

Sam said, "As a chiropractor is to a doctor?"

I said, "As an editor is to a sculptor. Or is it sculptor to editor?"

Sam said, "As green tea is to coffee?"

I said, "No, I've got it. A drag queen is to a halfback as an ascot is to a tie."

"That's it exactly," said Sam. "It's a style thing, not a moral thing."

I said, "Not nearly moral. Style isn't even an ethical thing."

"Until we attempt to alter it," said Sam. "Then, of course, we're into ethics."

"Oh, yeah," I said, "it looks like shallow water from here, but once we step in, we're over our heads. In no time at all, we're drowning in makeup policies and other moral imperatives."

Sam said, "We're diving in together, right?"

I didn't say anything. We'd already taken the plunge.

Sam said, "What are you thinking about?"

I said, "Aftershave, bikini briefs, scented hair conditioners, earrings and nipple rings, monogrammed towels, loafers with tassels, and the spine-tingling prospect of Scot dressing up for Halloween."

eight

Scot had one unmitigated virtue. He was an out-and-out slob. He left pencils on chairs, notebooks in the refrigerator, comic books in the hamper, toast on windowsills, and a ring of violet bubble scum in the bathtub. When he dressed himself, he treated his body as he treated any other surface—he let things accumulate.

By the time Nula turned up with pears and apples, it was nearly lunchtime. She didn't want to go shopping. Then Scot appeared. His visible layer involved blue cotton shoes with crepe soles, a pair of red corduroy bell-bottoms, the top half of his brown pajamas, Sam's sweater dashingly tied around his neck, and a white rubber rain helmet. He shook hands with Nula and thanked her for the wooden box of bathroom supplies—"They're adorable," he said—then he shyly excused himself, and when he returned from his bedroom he was carrying a clear plastic umbrella with a candy-cane handle.

Nula whispered, "He's killing me with the accessories." She put a pear in the pocket of her black oilskin slicker.

"There goes any hope of lunch." After she socked away a second pear, she said, "I hope Sam's coming."

"He is."

"Good," she said. "We're gonna need his credit line."

Seated like four normal people in Sam's car, we all felt squeamish. The fog we made inside the windows gave us something to do, but none of us knew what to say as we wiped away the evidence of our collective embarrassment. While we were crossing the river into Boston, Sam said, "Where should we start?"

I had four suggestions; three were notably strong on ties and one had a young men's department. Sam named two big department stores. Scot said he could probably find something he liked just about anywhere. Nula nixed the entire list. "Our only hope is Brooks Brothers."

Scot was surprisingly amenable to the tedium of trying on blue sweaters and chinos and button-down oxford-cloth shirts. He told everyone in the store that he'd been an orphan for a while in Baltimore, before he met his guardians, and then Nula was offered a chair and Sam got a free tie. I held the rain helmet and umbrella and scared away a lot of business. Sam found a great nylon poncho with a sufficient number of zippers and pouches to please Scot, but the real coup was a navy blue duffle coat. Scot was besotted by its complicated buttons—leather loops and wooden pegs—and its plaid flannel lining.

While Sam and Nula were finalizing the sale, Scot stood in front of the three-way mirror with the coat slung over his shoulders like a mink. "Oh, Ed," he said, "isn't it a dream? I can't wait to wear it with my new brown bucks."

A perfectly reasonable-looking lawyer who was trying out briefcases nearby said, "Who's in charge of the sissy?"

Scot froze. He let the coat drop to the floor.

I wanted to lance the guy with the candy-cane umbrella. I wanted to inflate Scot. I wanted to vindicate my own ambivalence about Scot's droopy posture and his too-high voice. I yelled, "Scot! That man just called me a sissy. What should I do?"

Scot came to life. "He called *you* a sissy?"

"And he's still looking at me funny," I said, and he wasn't the only one.

Scot picked up his coat and reached for my hand. "Oh, Ed. Just remember what Sam says. We don't have to live with him. He does."

The lawyer trailed us to the counter, where Sam and Nula were looking at me as if I were an abstract painting. The lawyer whispered, "I'm really very sorry," aiming his gaze at the cash register.

Sam said, "Apology accepted," and led us past the lawyer and out into the warm air and cold rain, the mixed blessings enjoyed by all Bostonians on that particular day.

Nula and Sam ate the pears on the way home, and Scot and I pawed through his new things. And maybe it was the way everything from Brooks Brothers matched every other thing, or maybe it was Scot's lingering joy at the inclusion of pink among the sanctioned colors for button-down shirts, but the car windows didn't fog up, and after we dropped Nula in the Square, Sam and Scot and I went home and ordered pizza and canceled all pending plans and resolutions.

Scot fell asleep midway through the unpacking and sorting and hanging of his haul. Sam went to his office for an hour. I called Theo, who was young and broke and grateful to have a half-time job with the most something magazine in the world, and thus willing to work afternoons for a while, which meant I could meet Scot after school until—until—

Time took off like a rabbit on a racetrack.

I didn't make it out of the gate.

I couldn't keep up, no matter how many early-morning hours I put in at the magazine. The afternoon was the fax-free zone at American *Figura*, and it was important for Nula and me to make hay while the Italians dined and drank and voted out another government.

Scot needed a proper playmate.

Scot needed a hobby, like wood-burning or needlepoint.

Scot needed a scoutmaster or a swim coach or a piano teacher.

Scot needed a dentist and a haircut and help with his homework.

Scot needed chores and an allowance and a savings account.

Scot needed to get rid of that umbrella and he had to start picking up his own damn comic books and he wouldn't be in school on holidays or during the Christmas and February and April vacations and then the summer sun was bearing down on me and Sam was standing in the doorway trying to remove one of the tea roses with his car key, and he said, "Hey, sissy, wanna be friends?"

My cup of tea.

nine

You can buy peace, but it is rather expensive. This makes the jewelry business a good one. Many a man has bought himself a month or two in diamonds and gold, and Tiffany can sell you a solid year.

Scot got a duffle coat and a poncho, and by Thursday Sam had to pick him up from school before lunch. His mineral-science partners had noticed, and then told Miss Paul, that Scot was wearing panty hose. Scot went silent, and on Friday he was forced into early retirement again, and Sam called me, and I met Miss Paul, who led me to the principal's office, where Scot was alone, slouched in the *You sit right here and wait while I call your parents* chair. He didn't see us immediately.

Miss Paul said, "The principal must have stepped out."

Scot was ready to step out, too. He snapped his compact shut, stuck it in the pocket of his pink shirt, and blinked demurely. His eye shadow was mint green, his lipstick dusty rose. He was still mute, and I didn't ask about his hosiery.

"He applied the makeup during lunch period." Miss Paul herself had selected a shimmery lip gloss and a rather severe brown eyeliner. I assumed that she had given hers a touch-up at lunch, as well.

I asked if the Parker Elementary School had a makeup policy.

Miss Paul smiled. She had a Cleopatra haircut, and she was shaped like a snowman, so everything she said had a tone of rueful jollity. "I don't think school rules anticipated this case. Shall we close the door for a minute?"

Scot whimpered as the door swung shut, and he began to cry, which allowed us to speak freely.

Miss Paul said, "I know what you're thinking. If girls can wear makeup—and they do—why shouldn't boys be allowed? And that might go for panty hose, too. Right?"

Cambridge.

"Actually," I said, "I was thinking about taking him home and drowning him like a cat in the bath."

"I'll check," said Miss Paul, "but I think the school does have a rule about that."

She cracked open the door and said, "I don't like to leave you alone, even when we're standing right outside, Scot. I know you're feeling all alone, but you're not alone."

She got an A-plus in deportment. She agreed to meet with Sam and me as soon as we could arrange it. And Scot walked home with his hand in mine.

Mildred Monterosso was shuffling around on her blue-stone patio when we passed, and she called out, "Boys! Slow down. I've got something for you."

We waited on the sidewalk, and when Mildred was close enough to see Scot's face, she said, "Run home and wash your face, and then come right back here. And bring one of the little shovels I sent over."

Scot zipped home.

I said, "I think we're gonna have a talk before Scot gets any more gifts, Mildred, if you don't mind."

She waved her fat hand at me and showed me what she had packed into her apron pockets. "Bulbs," she said, and she spoke fast to shut me up. "I bought about a thousand of them. I've planted them everywhere but my own head. Ran out of space. I got crocuses, yellow tulips, and a couple of stargazer lilies. It'll take him all weekend to get them in the ground per my instructions, what with the exacting depth measurements and the bone meal for fertilizer, and Eddie, I heard about him and the nylons and, I know—now this. Jesus, Mary, and Joseph, I know. But don't have too much to say to him about it, Eddie. Not just yet. Think before you speak. And someday I'll tell you all about Georgie Junior at that age. Make your hair fall out, that kid could."

Scot called from his bedroom window, "Am I allowed out, Ed?"

"Put on your blue jeans, Scot," I yelled. "And a long-sleeve tee shirt."

Scot called back, "Any color?"

Mildred said to me, "I think a lot of boys wanna try on nylons and bras. Really, I do."

I yelled, "Any color," and turned to Mildred. "Don't keep him too long, Mildred."

"Just long enough so he understands how to set the bulbs," she said. "I'll make him take notes."

"He'll like that," I said.

"I'll have him hold off on planting until tomorrow, so Sam can join in the fun." Mildred held up her hand, like a crossing guard.

Scot stopped short, ten feet away. His jersey was already untucked and one of his sneakers was untied.

Mildred smiled. She, too, approved of his disarray. "You're going to need a notebook and a good pen," she said, making it clear that some important business was about to be conducted.

Scot ran back into the house.

I didn't want to move.

Mildred shooed me away. "I just bought you an hour, Eddie. Go home now. And if you were thinking a cold beer might hit the spot, then maybe you're getting the hang of it."

ten

Having a child, I soon learned, is like having an open wound. People ask you about it. They give you advice and secret remedies. Friends tell you to ignore it for a while and see if it doesn't heal itself. Everyone assures you that it won't kill you. And then they show you their scars.

Greg Koester called midway through my free hour. He worked as a trust officer for a private bank in an office high atop the financial district, and he had a commanding view of Boston Harbor and the airport. Whatever he said from there sounded confident and wise. He thought Scot was advertising his losses. "That's the meaning of the makeup," Greg said, and I said, maybe, but I didn't think Scot had wanted anyone to see the panty hose, so was that subliminal advertising? "I don't think I've ever told you this," Greg said, and his voice trailed off as he closed his office door, and when he returned, he clicked me from his speaker to his handset. "When I was in third grade, my mother had a series of operations, and she was gone for months, and every day she wasn't at home, my father put on her housecoat to cook us dinner. Maybe Scot is just trying to preserve something from the past."

Before I could get my tie unknotted, Nula called to ask after "the little strumpet," and she threatened to tell me something about her own growing up that would shock me, and I asked her to hold off. "Well, if you start thinking Scot's the only psychotic kid on the block, let me know. I can certainly top a pair of nylons and some blush." And Marco was coming to town with Sylvia, the scariest of the Italians, and we were all having lunch at the Gardner without Eleanor on Tuesday, which probably meant Friday, so I should call my friend and get her to save us a table for the week.

And then it was Joan, who said she'd been trying to get me for half an hour because she was worried about me and Sam, and had she ever told me that Greg's mother went nuts when he was eight?

No, she hadn't, and she needn't, I added.

"I don't think Greg's likely to tell you, but I do think he'd want you to know, which is where I come in. Still, you'll have to act surprised if he ever decides to spill this particular bean. Anyway, when he was in third grade, they dragged her out of the house by her hair and locked her up for almost a year. Greg dressed up in her clothes." Joan paused. "I don't think they'd invented panty hose yet, but you get the picture. He wore her housecoat to bed every night until she came back. It's just not that unusual, Ed." And were Sam and I and Scot still going to Robert and Danny's for dinner on Saturday?

Yes, we were, assuming I was able to digest both versions of the housecoat. And my tie was still flopping at half-mast, but I was on a roll, so I dialed up Robert's office, figuring he would be with a patient, but he wasn't, and he wanted to hear all of the details, which, as usual, he absorbed and refused to analyze immediately, unlike everyone I knew who didn't have a degree in psychiatry, but he did tell me that their dog—like most pets, it had been named, as if the genetic confusion of breeding wasn't insult enough—had to be fitted with a special collar to stop him from chewing on his own shoulder, and did I know if Joan and Greg had decided to bring Hank because children were definitely invited. Danny and Robert had a surprise for everyone.

I hoped it didn't involve a test tube.

I called my sister in Chicago. She was an hour behind, and that seemed like my best bet of buying back some of the time I'd squandered. Nancy was surprised that I hadn't made Scot read her *Diana in Danger* series.

Reflexively, I said, "But they're for girls."

And Nancy said, "I thought you said he was drawn to girls' things."

"I'm not sure Sam and I want to supply him with the exotica, though." I was tired of explaining myself and trying to sound judicious, and it was probably nothing that a cup of coffee wouldn't have cured, but I couldn't grind beans and talk at the same time.

Nancy said, "Hmm," and I knew what she was doing. She was turning the case over to Diana, the adolescent sleuth with a keen eye for hypocrisy. "You'd buy him a soccer ball, but not a jump rope. Is that it?"

"Not a jump rope with plastic tassels on the handles, anyway," I said.

"Caitlin wears men's boxer shorts. She and her friends haven't worn lace panties since middle school."

"But Scot's the kind of kid other kids push down and kick because of the way he puts his hand on his hip."

Nancy/Diana said, "Maybe you underestimate kids."

This was lifeblood of Nancy's oeuvre, and I didn't want to kill her career.

But then Nancy said, "Bob and Timmy both have gold studs. I was a little worried at first, but you learn to trust your kids. I bet a lot of kids think Scot is cool, you know, a rebel."

And I realized I was going to spend the rest of my life grinding up pearls of wisdom and other sanctimonious gems, and I said, "In a lineup of boys with earrings, you'll know Scot. He's the one sporting the white daisies. Clip-ons. Piercing is way too scary. Look closely now, because that's a charm bracelet on his wrist, and beneath his button-down shirt you think you see the faint outline of a muscle tee shirt, but look again, Nancy. That's a pearl white camisole with needlepoint roses on the ribbing. And he'll keep his coat, thank you, and wear it like an evening wrap because there's a chill in the air today. He's got a white patent leather belt, and you're the Queen Mother for a Day, and you get to decide: Tell me, Nancy, should Sam and I buy him a matching pair of white Mary Janes?"

"The books *are* age-appropriate," she said, "and there's a website where he can talk to other kids about them. If you get him on-line, he won't have to worry about the way he looks."

Everyone had a virtual solution. And then Sam walked in, so I thanked Nancy for the checkered mugs and bowls and told Sam about the housecoat and the crocuses.

Sam nodded and waited for his water to boil. "Did you talk to anyone else?"

Scot was swinging on the tire in the backyard, singing "O Come All Ye Faithful."

"I talked to Robert briefly," I said.

Sometimes Sam is a stingy slot machine, and I have to empty my pockets to get back a dime. But when I dropped the Robert coin, I hit the jackpot. "Did you call the *Globe*, yet, Ed? The wire services?" His voice was steady, but he was having trouble settling on the proper teapot for the occasion, and when he chose the unbreakable little cast iron kettle, I knew there wasn't enough tea in Chinatown to save me. "At least we know the menu for tomorrow night's dinner," he said.

I didn't get it.

"Robert will serve up a psychoanalysis of Scot for everyone's delectation. And for dessert, he can prescribe a shot of thorazine." Sam, a proponent of mild brews, packed black tea into the pot as if it were tobacco in a pipe. He dropped in three pieces of star anise.

"I'm not looking for answers from Robert."

Sam said, "Or Mildred, or Nancy, or Greg?"

I needed coffee, but the damn beans were in the freezer, and then there was the scooping and grinding and counting, and I'd still be only halfway there. "I'm just looking for advice, Sam."

"Here's a piece of advice from a former kid: Don't make it so Scot has to live up to his most embarrassing moments."

"Maybe I need to know if I'm up to his most embarrassing moments."

Sam tasted his tea, and he looked startled, but he didn't back down.

Sam's way: Respect the kid's privacy.

Ed's way: Don't underestimate our friends.*

---

*Adapted from the *Diana in Danger* series.

Sam's way: Give the kid a break.

Ed's way: Give me a break.

Scot was singing "Jingle Bell Rock" with a country twang.

"One of us is right," said Sam. He drained a vat of orange lentils that had been soaking in water all day, mixed them up with a few handfuls of wheat berries, and then sautéed them with bits of onion and garlic, and when I saw him eyeing a waxy turnip that I'd tried to bury beneath the bananas in a big bowl on the counter, I almost cried uncle.

I knew that talking about Scot had yet to yield an antidote for any of his antics, but I also knew that silence was fertile soil for the seeds of shame.

Sam's way: Peel the turnip, "just to add a little sweetness."

Ed's way: Open a can of tomato soup, "just in case."

Scot stashed his bulbs and bone meal under a sofa in the living room, and when he came into the kitchen he took a long look at our long faces and volunteered to take a bath before dinner.

Sam stirred the stew.

I set the table.

Sam added pinto beans and chicken broth.

I made coffee.

Sam said, "He's always gonna smell good, that kid."

I said, "Sleeps through the night."

Sam stirred the tomato soup.

I said, "He's not a gifted crooner."

Sam said, "Couldn't carry a tune with a wagon."

Before dinner, Sam and I took turns initialing the time slots on a big calendar he'd brought home, and when we'd bargained our way through October, we taped it to the side of the refrigerator. There were a few empty afternoon spaces, and we figured we could fill them up with piano lessons or a sport Scot might be good at—archery, maybe, or jazzercise classes at the Y.

Scot ate soup and stew like a trouper, and he sat very still when Sam said we were going to discuss makeup and money after dinner.

"I'm sorry about the eye shadow," Scot said. He had slipped on a knee-length plaid flannel nightshirt after his bath, which had other implications on him.

Sam said, "No matter what, from now on, you're never leaving school early, Scot. Ed and I are meeting with Miss Paul next week. That's the rule. And no time out in the principal's office. You'll be sitting in class like everybody else. Understood?"

Scot said, "Understood," but his furrowed brow seemed to say, change of plans.

I was impressed, too. Sam was starting to put a little spin on the ball.

Scot was sent up to his room with a box to collect all of his makeup—and, yes, that included nail polish—and all the money he had stashed in jars and winter hats.

I rinsed the plates and pots and dropped them into the dishwasher while Sam stood beside me with a towel in his hands. "Every woman I worked on today was wearing makeup."

I said, "Women do."

Sam wisely ignored me and said, "It was like reading a series of complicated instructions. How to look at me: Notice, I have lips. Disregard my chin. Believe in my cheekbones." Sam shook it off, whatever it was. "Try to talk about this, and you're a fanatic. But try to send a little boy to school with some eyeliner, and you've got a social worker with a clipboard at your front door."

I said, "I've always thought makeup was morning prayers."

Sam smiled. "What was Scot praying for?"

"Forgiveness, I guess."

Sam said, "Is that why women do it?"

"It's why I'd do it. Wouldn't you? If you thought it would make the gods smile on you?"

Sam looked really sad suddenly. "It depends on who's in your pantheon."

"We know who they are, Sam. We don't name them. But there's a lot we do and a lot we don't do to make ourselves acceptable in their sight. I humble myself before them every day when I don't kiss you good-bye in the street."

Sam wiped his face with the dish towel, and was he crying? He was trying not to, but he was.

I said, "Oh, Sam," but I wanted to break a window in everyone's home. Look at this. Look at what you're doing.

In a too-high voice, Sam said, "It makes me think of Billy," and he shook his head and wiped his face again and blew out air and faked a smile. "I think he would have stuck around if Scot had been a different boy. I really do." He was sadder than I'd ever seen him, and his mouth was open, as if he might be able to say what he really meant, and then very quietly he did say, "It's all so much more than I ever wanted to know about Billy. And how Billy sees me."

Scot scampered down the stairs.

Sam turned to the sink and splashed cold water on his face.

I rubbed his back.

Scot said, "Is Sam sick?"

And I said, "He's fine now."

And Sam turned around and said, "Sometimes I feel sad about something, and it makes me feel better to tell Ed."

Scot said, "You're lucky Ed's here."

Sam said, "So are you," and he said it lightly as he picked Scot up and carried him into the living room.

I finished the dishes, and then Sam sent Scot to the kitchen to order up weak tea for everyone, and to bring me to my appointed place. One of the great luxuries of our home was our oversupply of sofas. We had two long gray ones and two short white ones set around a vast square table, and this arrangement promoted lounging and snacking and falling asleep with a book on your face.

Sam had rummaged through the shoe box of beauty aids, but now the lid was on it. He had rolled up the bills—more than eleven hundred dollars, as I found out later—and rubber-banded them.

Scot liked that.

The change was sorted into piles of pennies, nickels, dimes, and quarters.

"Tomorrow morning," said Sam, "we're going to the bank so Scot can open up his own savings account." He held up the wad of bills. "This is your money, and you are also going to be earning an allowance, and you'll need to keep track of it all."

The "all" in that sentence appealed to Scot.

"We're also going to buy four fantastic colored bottles with reliable tops, one for each kind of coin."

Scot said, "Who picks them out?"

Sam said, "You do, and you check with Ed and me to see if we have spotted another kind that is so great we want you to get it."

Scot said, "How much should we spend on them?"

Sam said, "Ed and I are paying for the bottles. And for a wallet so you have a place to carry dollar bills."

Scot said, "Can it have a zipper?"

Sam said, "Or snaps. For walking-around money. Pocket change."

Scot said, "A change purse."

Sam didn't even blink. "Yes."

And we all sipped tea, sealing the deal.

And then a grave silence settled in.

We sipped.

Scot tried not to look at the bulging shoe box of beauty aids on the table.

We sipped.

Scot scooted off his sofa and put his hand on the lid of the shoe box. "What'll we do about all this?"

Sam and I sipped.

Scot said, "Maybe we should just get rid of it, right?"

Sam said, "I don't think so. Not yet, anyway."

I said, "Oh?"

Scot was intrigued, too. "Maybe we could buy a better box for all of it tomorrow, and then keep it somewheres."

Sam put his elbows on his knees and held his face in his hands. He looked at Scot as if he'd known him forever. "I thought about you all day long, Scot. Since you came to live with Ed and me, I think about you all the time. So does Ed." He closed his eyes and smiled. And when he opened his eyes, he said, "It's so great you live here with us. When I'm on my way home, I can't wait to talk to you about school and how you're feeling and what's for dinner." Then Sam shook his head apologetically. "But there's something incredibly important I keep forgetting to tell you." Here, he inserted a very long pause.

Scot and I both wanted to scream, What? What did you forget? But we held our cool.

Sam said, "You're going to change. In the next few years, you're going to change a lot, Scot. You'll get taller and your feet will grow, and your arms and legs and shoulders will be amazingly different. It's happening every day, and you're so used to it that you won't even notice all the changes. But I will. Every day of your life, I will notice you. I will memorize you every morning, and you will be a picture on my heart wherever I go."

Scot bowed his head, and then he went farther and rested his forehead right on the table. He was sobbing.

Who wasn't?

Sam was relentless. "I am looking at you right now, Scot. You're here." Sam patted his heart.

Scot lifted his head to look at Sam's heart.

Sam said, "Ed and I are your guardians. And I gotta tell you, we love your red hair and your gray eyes and the way your face gets pink when you're embarrassed, and your neck, too, like right now."

Scot wiped his face on his plaid sleeves and said, "You sorta caught me by surprise."

"I know. And I know you have your mom's eyes, Julie's beautiful gray eyes."

There, I thought, someone finally said it.

Scot said, "She used to dye her hair."

Sam said, "People try out different styles once in a while. Like my silly beard. Or a haircut. Or some new clothes."

From a pile of newspapers, Sam pulled out the Sunday magazine and held up the picture of the man with the pink lipstick. "It's a matter of taste, I guess, but I'd have to say, I think he's better to look at without it." He held his finger across the lips, and it was true. Now we could really see the all of him.

Scot was riveted, but he was suspicious. "Take the finger away."

Sam unveiled the lips.

"Put it back." He never took his eyes off the page, but he wagged his hand in my direction, as if to say, Are you catching this? He said, "One more time?"

If Sam took this act into department stores, he could close down the cosmetic counters in a matter of minutes.

The makeup was packed into an empty red metal toolbox that Scot had found while ferreting around in the basement. It had a latch, and a lock, and he gave Sam the key. Sam told him he could have the key, without explanation, whenever he needed access. He just had to ask. Then the box went back to the basement.

Scot looked a little lost. I made popcorn, which helped. Sam put on some jazz, and that helped. I read. Sam did a crossword puzzle. Scot tried to get interested in a book, a magazine, and he even tried to fall asleep in Sam's lap. And then he said, "Some of that stuff in the box isn't mine. Some of it belonged to my mother."

Sam said, "Maybe we ought to keep it in your room, then."

Scot said, "I think so," and he effected the transfer in a flash.

When he settled back into his sofa, I watched him tuck something under a throw pillow.

Sam put the key on the table. "Do you think you should keep this for now?"

Scot weighed the risks. "Maybe you should just let me know where it will be."

Sam said, "For tonight, right there."

Scot said, "Or maybe just up in your bedroom is better." He hesitated, and then said, "Do we have any Scotch tape?"

I said, "In the kitchen, in the drawer with the pens."

"Thanks. Just so I know."

He waited for a decent interval and then he slipped away with his secret. A few minutes later he returned without it, and a few minutes later Sam carried him upstairs, and a few minutes later Sam was snoring on his sofa, and a few minutes later so was I.

eleven

On Saturday morning, Scot joined me in the bathroom, and we brushed our teeth together. He said, "Should we let Sam sleep?" I nodded. He trailed me to the kitchen. He got us a couple of mugs, and I poured water into the stupid coffee machine and stared at it, as if it ought to know the drill by now. Scot selected a box of cereal for himself and handed me the coffee beans from the freezer. He kept the door open for a while, and when I turned to tell him to shut it, I finally noticed the picture he'd taped to the freezer door.

It was Julie. She had bangs, and she looked hungry and wry, like a cover girl. She was holding a paintbrush. Behind her was something bright. A sunny window, maybe, or a large lamp, or her hopes. She was wearing her pearls.

"We could look for a frame for that today," I said.

Scot said, "Really?"

"It's something we're all going to want to have for a long time."

Scot said, "Forever."

61

I didn't know how far to go. I said, "Thanks for hanging it up so we can all see it. We'll have to figure out where it will look best."

"Anywhere's fine." Scot added milk to his cereal. "Mostly, it'll be for our guests to look at. And for you. Me and Sam will have it memorized."

twelve

Sam and Scot wore chinos, white shirts, blue sweaters, and sneakers into Harvard Square, and they held hands. I wore jeans, a black jacket, and it was windy, so I couldn't hear much of anything they said until we were in a store, where they behaved like aristocrats, picking up things, comparing them unfavorably to other things, and wondering why no one made the things they imagined and desired. Eventually, they did find some serviceable jars and a wooden frame for Julie, and I carried the bags to the bank, where they sat in soft leather chairs, and I stood beside them like a bodyguard while Art Timilty, the clinically depressed assistant manager who was wearing matching watches, one on either wrist, filled out forms and read the disclaimers aloud in a voice modulated by the foreknowledge that no one would be listening.

When Art stood to go find a passbook, Scot said, "How come you need two watches?"

Art said, "I'm ambidextrous," and left.

Sam said, "That means he can write with his left hand and his right."

Scot said, "At the same time?"

And then Joey Morita turned up. He stood directly in front of Scot's chair, like a supplicant. "Hi, Scot. My mom said I could come over." He turned and pointed to the long line of customers waiting to speak to the one human teller in the bank. His belly bulged out of his open jogging jacket, and we could see his orange crossing-guard harness.

Scot said, "You're not on duty today, you know."

Joey said, "Nope," and he waved at me.

I waved back.

Sam introduced himself, shook Joey's hand, and Scot said, "I told you about him," as if Joey had committed a faux pas by not recognizing Sam.

Joey said, "I like your sweaters, guys."

Scot said, "They match."

Joey said, "I have a blue sweater at home."

Scot almost said something mean—I could see it in his legs, which were swinging, as if he might suddenly kick Joey in the knees—but he looked at Sam and simply nodded his head.

Joey said, "You look like you're on the same team."

Scot said, "It's a style."

Joey adjusted his strap and spoke directly to his belly. "You look good in that style."

Mrs. Morita spotted her son, and then she recognized me, and then Scot. She didn't come right over. She took a couple of big breaths first, and then she blew by me and shook Sam's hand, preventing him from standing. Her first name was Liz, and she was not much taller than her son, and maybe half his weight. She smiled at me, as if we shared a

sad secret, and she waved at Scot and said, "Hello, there."
Then she ran out of steam.

Sam said, "I guess the boys are getting to be friends."

"Or so it seems," said Liz.

Sam was confused and amiable, a combination I can
never muster, and he invited her to our house "for tea sometime," to inspect the premises, presumably, and allow Joey to
come over and play.

Joey said, "Please, Mom?"

Scot pretended not to care, but his legs betrayed him
again. He coiled the left leg around the right one as he await-
ed her verdict.

Liz said, "I'd like that," and she relaxed a little. It wasn't
relief, though. It was a concession. She looked at Joey's belted belly and Scot's double-knotted legs, and anyone could
see that their friendship was manifest destiny. You could call
them outcasts, or you could call them the accidental Lewis
and Clark of kid world, a couple of frightened explorers
clinging to each other to keep from falling off the map.

Art Timilty returned with a passbook, Liz grabbed Joey's
hand, Sam stood up, and Scot imitated his good manners;
and then Joey lunged, hugged Scot, and kissed him on the
lips. Before any of us knew what to do, Joey said, "I like you,
Scot."

Scot went purple and swooned back into his soft chair. "All
right, already," he whispered, "now good-bye."

Art Timilty opened a desk drawer, but he saw that he
couldn't climb in, so he checked the time twice.

Liz Morita looked at me reprovingly.

Sam said, "Maybe you'll want to call me."

Liz shook her head. "Soon, if you don't mind. I'm a little
over my head here. Tomorrow?"

Sam nodded.

I said, "Good-bye, Joey. I'm glad we ran into you today." The kid wasn't a criminal. A masher maybe, but I admired his impetuousness. No one else did.

Liz grabbed his hand.

Sam turned with concern—maybe sympathy—to Scot.

Scot shrugged.

Art said, "Super duper. Super duper."

It was an ambidextrous cry for help for help.

Sam gently pulled the passbook from Art's hand. "Is that for us?"

Scot said, "What time is it?" This was bait.

Art twisted his wrists and raised his hands like a sheriff wielding six-shooters.

Sam sharply said, "It's time to go, Scot."

But Art wasn't offended. "It's nearly noon," he said, and he smirked at Scot before he said, "And nearly noon." He shook our hands. "Thank you, gents. And you, young man, you come straight to my desk here if you have any questions about how your fortune is faring. Or what time it is."

Scot was impressed by the mildness of the rebuke, and so was I.

Sam said, "Thank you."

Scot said, "Thank you, sir," and slid off his chair, trailing Sam, and trailed by me to Sam's office, where I was asked to take my shirt off, lie down, and, for Scot's benefit, absorb a little radiation. Sam was proving to Scot that X rays didn't hurt. Then I was palpated—a little dismissively, I thought—and Sam gratuitously cracked my back twice, again for Scot's edification. Sam had long since worked out the kinks—subluxations, if Sam was talking—in my spine, though when I stood up one of my ears did pop and everything seemed louder. I didn't report the miracle, however; sudden feelings of wellness made Sam suspicious, and he would have spent weeks grilling me about ligaments and tear ducts and joints. He believed in a body's innate intelligence, a sort of CIA that operated the central nervous system, and his job was to decode the cryptograms patients reported: Earache? Nerve interference. Sore, cold feet? Circulatory reaction to vertebral dislocation. Migraine following an adjustment? Predictable symptom of chemical detoxification as released energy cleanses the body.

Sam asked Scot to take off his sweater and shirt.

Scot said, "I'd like a little privacy, Ed." He was sitting on the wooden ledge of the tea cabinet, and he was framed like a painted figure by the shiny glass doors that loomed behind him. He looked like a child martyr—or an angel, had I been in a better mood.

I buttoned my shirt.

Sam said, "Maybe Ed can make us some tea."

Maybe Ed could mop the floor with Scot. I said, "Maybe I'll stop by the office and meet you at home."

Scot pulled his sweater over his head and held it there. He undid one button with his free hand. He said, "Ed! Good-bye, already."

"Scot!" Sam winced at the volume of his own voice.

Scot whimpered, and then his sweater drooped down around his neck, and like wax from a candle, he dripped right off the counter. He was trying to cry, but he interrupted the effort to say "I'm sorry" with his face to the floor.

Sam said, "Just stand up, Scot. No one is angry. We just want you to—"

What did we want? I hoped Sam would fill in the blank.

Scot stood up and leaned against Sam's leg.

Sam looked at me encouragingly.

My innate intelligence system was broadcasting static.

Sam casually stripped off Scot's sweater, and Scot dutifully unbuttoned his shirt, and suddenly I was in the odd position of being appeased, as if I had wanted to see Scot half naked.

We were all a little ashamed of ourselves. We weren't exactly a family, but we shared a familiar feeling. Over time, in our peculiar lives, some of the shame of being ourselves had stuck to each of us, and it seemed to be the only glue holding us together.

My other ear popped. I could hear to Padua, to the sainted and secular sanctuary of the Scrovegni Chapel, where Giotto painted the Last Judgment on the entrance wall, so it is behind you by the time you enter. It's the right perspective, but I couldn't put it into words.

I tapped Scot on the head, patted Sam's arm, and shuffled toward the door.

Sam said, "Joan and Greg are driving us all to dinner. Around six?"

Scot said, "I'll carry home the bags, Ed."

Giotto said, "Judgment. Behind you. Get it?"

I circled back and kissed them both, and we all turned pink.

thirteen

On Saturday evening, that blush of pink deepened into crimson, and like the autumn leaves above us, we couldn't shake off the color. It darkened. We were changing. We were being changed.

We didn't eat dinner with Robert and Danny, and a week later Danny called me at work and told me they'd bought the summer house in Provincetown in which Sam and I had spent many happy hot August days with them and other friends whose names I now occasionally print on a postcard or pronounce at night, when I need to speak to the dead.

"That was the big announcement we never got around to making. We were going to ask you and Sam to buy into it with us," Danny explained, "and we figured maybe even Joan and Greg, too, but—."

I said, "But not Scot."

Danny said, "Don't be crazy, Ed. Robert and I love Scot."

"Really?"

Danny said, "Really. Of course."

I said, "You want him for a few years?"

Danny said, "I think you're going to find he's hard to give away, Ed. Like a fondue pot."

A week earlier, I might have laughed. A few weeks before that, I probably would have been insulted. But the truth was that Scot would really enjoy a fondue party.

We hadn't seen Danny and Robert since that abortive Saturday evening, and Robert probably wanted to keep that streak going. Their place in the city was designed and decorated in the raw-materials style of the eighties—one giant room of exposed brick, beveled plate glass, black leather, polished chrome, and bunches of tulips in galvanized tin cans. Scot walked in, took one look at the spiral staircase that pirouetted up to the loft bedroom and the only bathroom, and he started to sweat. He unpegged his blue duffle coat. Above the collar of his white button-down shirt, Scot had knotted a shiny yellow and green scarf around his neck, something Mildred Monterosso might have worn over hair curlers. It wasn't an ascot; it was sportier than that, tomboyish, a neckerchief that made you think of bobby socks and Doris Day and the butch glamour of those platinum blondes who starred in movies with Rock Hudson, Montgomery Clift, and James Dean—actors who became famous for their smoldering looks, which was the popular way of saying that Doris worked like a wet blanket on their passions.

You're a decent person. You're among friends. What do you say to a boy in a neckerchief?

Sam didn't say anything. He had a policy of not embarrassing Scot in public.

I didn't say anything. I had a policy of not embarrassing Sam in public, and after we'd planted Mildred's bulbs and showered, I had inspected Scot's bedroom for neatness, and Sam was supposed to approve Scot's outfit for the evening.

Joan and Greg didn't say anything, either. Joan had a policy: When other people's kids do something bad or humiliating, you pretend not to notice. It is just as rewarding to gloat later on, in private.

Besides, Hank was cranky.

Robert and Danny were in the worst position. This was their first physical encounter with Scot, which for most people turned into an encounter session with themselves. You wanted to laugh, only you didn't want to be a person who laughed at the girlie boy. You figured he wanted to be noticed, to be complimented on his attire, only you knew that was not really the history of your own fashion disasters; you yourself had once worn that flashy silk shirt with the large, floppy collar, and you'd kept your coat on at the party.

That was just the first split second in the atomic reaction.

Then the dog bounced by a few times. It was a big black poodle wearing a white plastic funnel over its head, and still nobody broached the topic of neckwear. Danny clamped his arm around the dog's middle. I'd never noticed it before, but they had the same hair. He kindly reminded everyone that the dog "sometimes nips people," and Robert defensively added, "only if their hands are hanging down."

Joan picked up Hank and handed him to Greg.

Hank wisely put his head on his father's shoulder and closed his eyes. Greg said, "I think maybe he has a fever."

Danny dragged the dog into the kitchen area, where it whined and gulped and tried to snag the funnel off its head with its front paws. Scot pressed back against the exposed brick and raised his hands over his head. He glanced around the vast, open territory and said, "I wish you had more walls in here."

Robert said, "Another animal lover in the family." This was directed at me. I had a history of hating the dog, according to Robert, though the truth was that I had a history of hating people who kept pets in apartments and invited me into the cage.

Joan and Greg drifted to a sofa. They'd been conducting a semi-private fight since we got into their car, and as far as I could tell, one of them did and one of them did not want to have another kid, and apparently the question had to be resolved this evening. Hank started to cry, and Greg said something and moved to a chair of his own, and then everybody heard Joan say, "At least we're out of the goddamn house."

Danny yelled, "I'm opening wine. Red or white?"

Joan yelled, "Both."

We hadn't taken off our coats.

Robert bent toward Scot and extended his hand, "Hello, Scot. We haven't really met yet. I'm Robert."

Scot shook his hand. "Hello. Why do you have a dog that likes to bite?"

Robert stayed stooped over, as if that might make Scot relax, and he said, "He doesn't bite."

Scot said, "Whatever," and he went pigeon-toed and pressed his knees together, which made him even shorter.

Robert squatted and said, "You can trust me."

The dog barked, and Scot looked at the ceiling.

Robert said, "If we talk about something else, I bet you'll feel more comfortable. Maybe you and I could choose what kind of pizza to order."

Scot said, "Are you the doctor or is Danny?"

Robert said, "I am."

Scot said, "Please don't stand so close to me. It's bad manners."

Small as he was, and high as those ceilings were, Scot had raised the temperature in the room to a simmer. That's his gift: he's catalytic.

Robert said, "Pardon me," and he meant, "Kiss my ass, kiddo," and he backed up too far and bumped into a ginger jar of umbrellas, which tipped over and cracked.

The dog yipped its approval.

Sam said, "Scot—"

And Scot said, "You said I'm not supposed to tell the doctor any of our business."

Sam had said it more subtly, but he had said it.

Robert waited for Sam to deny the charge.

No matter how strenuously Joan denies it, I will always believe that she pinched Hank's thigh to make him scream at this juncture. She stood up and said, "I think it's his ears. They're infected."

Robert kicked the umbrellas and the shards of pottery toward the wall. And he might have given a signal—I didn't see it, but the dog suddenly sprinted toward Scot as if he'd just been waiting to get a clear shot at him.

Scot spread himself like mortar against the wall, I stepped toward him, and Sam raised his fist and yelled, "Sit," and the dog did, just like that, and then he shuffled toward Sam and wanted to lick his shoes, which Robert would not permit.

Scot put his hands over the zipper of his chinos. The stain was spreading. I grabbed him and ran him up to the bathroom, and he really didn't leak much on the way, which isn't easy, and I congratulated him as I doused the wet patch he'd left on my shirt.

"I look like a baby," he said.

I persuaded him to add water to the problem. "We'll just say we turned on the faucets and got splashed. Both of us."

He watched me and nodded his approval. As I bent and doused his trousers, he brushed my hair back from my forehead and said, "Are you having a good time tonight, Ed?"

He made me love him at moments, and those moments had a way of making me forget myself. I adjusted his neckerchief so the little tails stuck out on the side like they were supposed to. "Not really," I said.

Scot said, "I think I'm too little to like it here, maybe. There's a lot of booby traps."

We were both ready to go home. And as we tentatively approached the scary spiral staircase, Scot said, "I'm glad you hate dogs, Ed. I thought I was the only one."

Many apologies were exchanged, and everyone was forgiven, and no pizza was ordered, and we left Robert and Danny to resume the life they had chosen many years before, though never more wholeheartedly than they chose it that Saturday night. We didn't stop to eat because of Scot's pants and my shirt and everyone's mood, and when we stood outside the Koester's house on the corner of Finn Street, we couldn't figure out whether to stick together or split up. We were all looking at Louisa Bamford's empty home, wondering who would plug up that particular hole in our hearts.

Sam said, "We'll be surprised, whoever happens to buy the place."

Joan said, "Hope they're one of us, whoever we are." She suggested pizza and a video, and Scot voted yes, but he wanted to change his pants first. He said he'd lost his house key somewhere between the dog and the bathroom, so he took mine, and Sam told him he had to take a quick shower before we did anything.

Greg said, "Hank's asleep."

Joan said, "Before you? That's a first."

They had a fight to finish. I said, "Did Scot leave his bedroom light on?"

Everyone looked. The light was on. Then the room went dark. We didn't say anything. After a few seconds, the light went on again.

Sam said, "That must be our cue."

The four of us exchanged more apologies, and I wondered if that's how most people with children end up saying good night.

On the curb near our fence, Ryan Burlington and a black-haired beauty were necking. Ryan's eyes were open, and he winked and waved as we passed. When we were inside, Sam said, "Oh, to be young and not in love." I went upstairs to put on a bathrobe, and Sam ordered a large plain pizza, and Scot stayed in the shower until it arrived. I noticed that his bed was a mess, which was not only against the rules but almost worthy of Goldilocks. Who'd been sleeping in Scot's bed? I really had checked it before we left. Why did he tear it apart when he got home?

I didn't want to know. For one night, I wanted Danny and Robert's life, a life with one well-made bed, a life with feta cheese and figs on the pizza. I pulled Scot's sheets and blanket together and turned out the light, and I didn't mention it to Scot or Sam. I didn't want to set off yet another round of apologies.

It was a sorry mistake.

fourteen

When things went wrong, which is to say whenever Scot skipped into the room, Sam had a philosophy to fall back on, and I had Nula.

Sam actually believed that he could crack Scot's back into a straight line and release his innate energy. I knew Sam's hands pretty well. He could do it, all right. He had straightened me out. When we met, I wasn't perfect partner material. I was a struggling artist and most of the struggling I did was fairly artless; for instance, I was getting along way too well with my landlord. And even after I'd moved in with Sam and he began to audit my fidelity account, I posted some profound deficits. His record wasn't perfect, either, at least during our first year. He'd confessed to me about one night at a conference with his former boyfriend, though at the time I considered that sort of thing a genuine social obligation.

It took me several years, and a few really painful adjustments at Sam's hands, to figure out that monogamy is a choice you only make once. It was just like my ears popping; it just came to me.

"Universal intelligence," Sam said. "You were born with it. It's innate. But you'd twisted up your life so badly that it couldn't circulate inside you."

But for the next few months, my circulatory system lit up nerves I didn't know I had, and I grew snoopy and suspicious. I accused Sam of sleeping with all the men who weren't busy sleeping with me anymore. I wanted descriptions of his clients, and details like a nipple ring and clipped chest hair made me jealous enough to sign up for a very expensive life-drawing class. Sam's faith in me was unshaken. When I was at my worst, he'd slap me down on his table, fiddle and press, and he'd always come up with a startling sound effect for his finale, until one day I stood up from the table, and I understood that I would never know if Sam had chosen me and me alone. I hadn't chosen Sam because he didn't want anyone else. I hadn't chosen him because I didn't want anyone else. I'd chosen him because I wanted one reliable, certain source of happiness in my life that was mine, and mine alone to administer.

Sam is my cup of tea, but sometimes you're just too tired to wait for the water to boil.

Monogamy is my morphine drip.

But self-medication is a risky business. Ask Julie. I knew Sam could make Scot stand up straight, but I wasn't sure Scot had the innate intelligence to choose Sam over smack.

"Scot can't choose between a baseball jacket and a blouse." Nula was sitting across from me at our desk. She hadn't removed her father's camel hair coat, which made her look like a hand puppet. "He can't decide whether to part his hair on the right or the left."

It was a gray day, and cold, and we were waiting for Sylvia and Marco, who were taking us to lunch. It had been a week of recriminations with them, and Marco was particularly bitter about the distance from Boston to New York. "The advertising agency is in New York," he told Eleanor Covena, expecting her to deny it. Eleanor said, "You hired the agency," and Marco said, "As usual, you know the correct answer to my question, Eleanor, but still my problem is not solved." Eleanor Covena had called in sick again, and Theo was taking a nap in one of the bedrooms below us. He would have slept better in his tiny apartment, where there was a bed, but he needed the money.

Nula said, "Did Scot make his bed this morning, or did you?"

I hadn't checked. I'd fallen into an evening inspection regime. Scot had learned to dawdle in the morning just long enough to make me leave the house before he did, and then he'd run down Finn Street and catch me at the corner. I thought he liked to be the one who locked up the house. I said, "I don't know why I've become such a stickler about the bed."

Nula said, "Maybe you believe people ought to clean up their own messes."

I said, "Exactly."

Nula said, "And you don't exactly need the forces of Universal Intelligence coursing through your body to figure out how to make your own damn bed."

I said, "Right."

"Which doesn't explain why you make his bed every other day. And I'm freezing. I have to turn on a heat lamp." Nula switched on the nearest of four swivel desk lamps that we'd bolted to our tables, and she stuck the white metal shade on her head like a cap. "When we go to lunch, I'm ordering a real space heater."

I said, "What is making the bed? It's meaningless."

Nula said, "If you don't have to make it, it is."

And then Sylvia appeared. "Marco is too discouraged to join us for lunch. The party at your little Gardner Museum had to be postponed. We are willing to pour money into the American edition, but we're not going to invite people to a party if they don't bother to renew their subscriptions. I see Eleanor is ill again. That is a disease we will soon cure." Sylvia was a Brit, but as a teenager she'd exported herself to Italy, where her height was not considered a breach of etiquette. She knew nothing about sculpture, magazines, or how to make friends. Marco liked to travel with her because she was monumental and mean. She was six feet tall, and she wore very high heels—coffee-table legs, really—so she was always coming at you like a downhill skier.

I stood up.

Sylvia said, "Don't greet me. Everyone in America has the flu, and I don't want it. Unless you were standing up to go downstairs and do something about that homeless man on the second story."

Nula said, "We need heat."

Sylvia said, "I've brought you four new portable computers. They're downstairs. Who is that man?"

Nula said, "I don't use a computer."

Sylvia stayed in the door frame. She was wearing a white jumpsuit, which somehow made it clear that we weren't going to lunch. "I took your advice and looked at the Giotto, Ed. It's the only one in America?"

I said, "We have five. But the Gardner's is the best."

She said, "It's not authentic, of course. Not even signed. You should come to Padua. Both of you. The moment you walk into the Scrovegni Chapel, you will see your stupidity."

Nula said, "Did you at least like the two van Goghs? They're signed."

There were no van Goghs at the Gardner, of course.

Sylvia said, "Not first-tier, but fun to look at. Yes, those two are worth having."

Nula had done this for me and for Boston and for Isabella Stewart Gardner and for Giotto, and I didn't say so, but it was just like making the bed for Scot and for Sam and for peace in the world.

fifteen

You hang a picture on your living room wall, you tilt your head, you adjust the picture a bit, and you walk away. Someone else walks by, tilts his head the other way, adjusts it a bit, and he walks away. You do this often enough, you figure, and it will be straight, or it will look straight, or at least straight enough, or there's always tomorrow, and one day the nail pops out of the plaster, the frame cracks, the glass shatters, and you have a hole in the wall and a picture that needs to be reframed.

But for a while there, you really believed one of you was going to get it right.

I must have made that bed fifteen times over the next six weeks, and as I was the purser, this meant Scot never once collected his weekly allowance, which we had set up as an all-or-nothing payment plan. Apparently Scot's credit was good at the thrift shops to which he dragged Joey Morita on their way from school to Super Computing classes at the library, because he often tried to sneak out in the morning wearing a new hair net or a crocheted vest or a Swiss-dot curtain he'd mistaken for a scarf. Whenever I asked him to account for a new item, he'd say, "This old thing? I've had it for ages, Ed," and he did have stuff from his former life stuck in coffee cans and tucked into bookcases all over the house, and even he didn't know where half of it was. Often he'd put on a pair of pants and delight himself by finding a couple of dinner napkins or a picture he drew in second grade.

Joey Morita was a true-blue friend to Scot. He joined in all of Scot's after-school activities—computers, the Mineral Club, and ¡Hola!, where Scot learned very few Spanish words but acquired an interest in the Grand Canyon, which, despite evidence I provided to the contrary, Scot continued to think of as home to many talented Mexican pottery-makers living in "caves that were designed by bees." He was getting straight A's in school. Joey's grades had improved, too, and Miss Paul and Liz Morita both credited Scot.

"He's an avid reader," Miss Paul told us at parent-teacher night.

Sam said, "We don't have a television."

Miss Paul treated this as a non sequitur. "That's okay, for now," she said, as if maybe we couldn't afford one and she didn't want us to feel bad about it.

Sam said, "I think that's why he's such a reader."

Miss Paul hadn't finished. "But we do have a media curriculum in the third and fourth quarters. We teach the children how to be critical participants instead of passive viewers."

Sam said, "You make them watch TV?"

Miss Paul laughed and touched Sam's forearm. "It's not a struggle."

Sam said, "Not like with books."

"Exactly."

Sam started to ask his clients and colleagues about private schools. I couldn't tolerate the idea of separating Scot from his only friend. I started to help Joey and Scot with their homework. At Liz Morita's request, Sam talked to Joey and Scot about sexuality and the hierarchy of affectionate gestures, and like most gay kids, Joey was happy to know that he wasn't the inventor of the boy-boy business, and from then on he abstained from kissing, except when he got really excited—like when they were on the swing together—and even then he aimed for the cheek and promised he wouldn't do it again without permission.

When I asked Scot how the sex lesson had gone, he asked if boys ever shaved their legs.

I said they didn't usually. That's right, isn't it?

He asked for a list of other girl-only items and habits, and as Sam had taken all the easy, biological ones, I was left with buttons on the left side, white-rimmed sunglasses (Don't you think? Go to the drugstore.), and high heels. But I went further. I said, "Do you know why you like girls' things?"

Scot said, "Don't you like them?"

"Not to wear," I said.

Scot was lying on his stomach on his sofa, and his arms were folded under his chest. "Miss Paul says it confuses the other kids if I do something like wear my charm bracelet or mince my words."

"What do you suppose she means?"

Scot liked Miss Paul, and so did I, but I needed some hard facts to convince Sam to keep Scot in her classroom. Scot said, "I suppose she means I have to learn to respect other people."

Blue ribbon to Miss Paul. But I needed more. I said, "I'm not sure I understand."

Scot said, "She means, if something like a bracelet is so important that you have to wear it once in a while, you better not show off or pout in class that day, or else you've got it coming to you."

I said, "Do the other kids do mean stuff to you?"

"Only behind my back. Ever since Tony started being my friend, there's a lot less trouble for me and Joey and our gang."

Scot was a deceptively deep pond. You never knew what you might reel in. I had two new facts on the line. Tony, the younger of the bald Burlington boys, had become Scot's friend. That merited an investigation. But good news first. "You have a whole gang of friends? That sounds like fun. Who are they?"

Scot said, "Kids like me and Joey. Some of them need operations and stuff."

"Girls or boys?"

Scot had to think before he said, "Mostly it's just me and Joey and a girl named Carla who has stomach problems and has to be allowed to leave the room whenever she feels like it. And Anton, but he's absent a lot and probably is gonna be left back again. He's thirteen, and Miss Paul is afraid he's gonna be old and gray before she gets him to high school."

"And what about Tony?"

Scot paddled his feet against the arm rest. "Tony's a sixth-grader, so he's never gonna like me, but Ryan made him promise to take care of any kids who make trouble for me. He's able to frighten kids by just the way he says their last name. Also, everybody knows he orders weapons from magazines."

I tried and failed to get anything out of Scot about the price he was paying for protection. Ryan Burlington, the bigger one, visited religiously, every Sunday morning, and he talked to Scot on the back stoop. Sam suspected Scot was slipping Ryan something to keep him coming and to keep Tony in line, but all Scot had to offer were fresh bagels and secondhand baubles, and Ryan usually brought his own potato chips, and his taste in jewelry ran to the simpler side—safety pins and rivets.

Scot acted insulted whenever Sam asked why Ryan was so friendly, and after the police turned up at the Burlington home two nights in a row, Scot flitted around the living room windows like a bird trying to escape, and he refused to believe that neither Sam nor I knew what the cops were after, and he finally accused Sam of conspiring to "spoil the best thing that ever happened to me." He pouted through dinner that night, and when Sam told him he had to go to his room until he could control his emotions, Scot stood up and screamed, "You're just like Ryan's stepfather. You think I'm a sissy and Ryan's a drug addict and you want to put everybody in concentration camps."

It was a botched version of a lecture Ryan had delivered. That's all we knew.

Sam had the wit to say, "Concentration camps?"

Indignantly, Scot said, "You know what I mean."

Sam said, "I don't."

Scot slapped his hands on his thighs. "Tell me another one." He waited, and when he was thoroughly disgusted with our inability to respond, he said, "The Nazis? Like, who do you think dropped the atom bomb?"

Miss Paul was out of the running for history prizes. And though Scot didn't know it, he was pretty far down a road that led to either a private school or a reform school.

Sam said, "Scot, it was Americans who dropped the atom bomb."

This headline clearly did not jibe with the story Scot had been reading. He did his best to recover. "On China?"

Sam looked at me.

I said, "Japan."

Sam said, "What I really want to know, Scot, is do you honestly believe Ed and I want to hurt you?"

Scot was standing about ten feet from the table. He knew he was already way out of bounds. "No."

"Did we ever call you a sissy?"

"No."

That was the history. What followed was unprecedented.

Sam pushed his chair back from the table. "What is a sissy, Scot?"

Scot was sniffling, but he knew this was serious. "A boy," he said.

Sam said, "What kind of a boy?"

Scot said, "A boy who acts like a girl."

Sam said, "Is that the kind of boy you are?"

"Sometimes. Yes."

Sam said, "On purpose?"

Scot hesitated. "Yes?"

Sam said, "I'm asking you."

"Yes."

Sam said, "Does it make you happy?"

Scot said, "I don't know."

Sam said, "Does it make you happy?"

Scot said, "It makes me feel okay."

Sam said, "Okay?"

Scot said, "Okay, like a little happy and little not so happy, but okay." Scot was calm, and he said, "Can I sit down now?" He didn't move.

Sam said, "Like when you put on that bracelet with the charms on it."

Scot said, "You mean, why do I like it?"

Sam said, "Does it make you happy? Do you say to yourself, Now I am happy?"

Scot smiled, "Not like that I don't."

Sam smiled. "What do you say?"

Scot said, "Why are you all of a sudden so interested in what I say to myself, if you don't mind me asking?"

Sam said, "I think you're unhappy, and I want to help."

Scot looked at his wrist. "I say to myself, I got this in Baltimore from a lady who used to stay with us sometimes. Her name was Alex. She said I wasn't like all the boys she ever fell in love with. They were after her jewels, so I should take it."

Sam said, "And?"

Scot held his wrist to the light. "I say, the kids at school are gonna give me a hard time today, but tell me something I don't know."

Sam said, "Anything else?"

Scot said, "Don't go getting any big ideas when I say this, but lately I sort of wonder why the charm bracelet isn't on the Forbidden List. With the makeup and ladies' nylons."

Sam said, "I don't want you to go cold turkey."

Scot pursed his lips. "You think I'm addicted?" He clamped onto the line of Sam's gaze and slid across the room like a funicular. He landed in his chair.

Sam said, "People sometimes get addicted to things. They start to depend on them to change the way they feel. I don't want you to think you need a special shirt or a certain pair of shoes or a bracelet to be happy."

Scot didn't say anything. He looked stricken. He stole a glance at Julie, who was hanging on the wall behind me. He said, "I think I need a cool drink."

Sam poured him some water.

Scot looked at me over the rim of his glass as he gulped, and then he banged it down like a beer on a bar. He said, "Okay. How about you, Ed?" He was gripping the seat of his chair. "You might as well let me have it, too."

"Do you think I act like a girl, Scot?"

Scot relaxed his grip. "Really?"

I said, "Really."

He said, "Maybe when you kiss me? Or when we go to the museum and you get so excited about the pictures?"

"Do you think I'm a sissy?"

Scot said, "Is it a trick question?"

"No."

Scot said, "Well, no, I don't think you are one."

"So sometimes I seem to act like a girl, but I'm not a sissy?"

Scot said, "Maybe it's okay to act like a girl sometimes."

"How are we going to figure this out, then?"

Scot said, "You better just ask Sam."

Sam said, "I don't know, Scot. Do all girls act the same?"

Scot was definitive about this. "No way. My friend Carla throws up all the time, and she'd not afraid to look at it. Most of the boys are. And Nula. She doesn't even bother to shave herself anywheres."

Sam said, "This is complicated, isn't it?"

Scot said, "May I ask a different question? Can we put words on the Forbidden List?"

Sam nodded.

Scot said, "Should we just forbid it?"

Sam said, "Sissy?"

Scot said, "Yes, please. I don't think we need to say it any more, do you?"

Sam said, "I can live without it."

I said, "I'm happy to give it up."

And the next day, Scot wrapped the charm bracelet in a lady's handkerchief and left it in Mildred's mailbox. He wrote a note.

Dear Mrs. M.,

You may wear this whenever you want and have it. It is mostly best for cocktail parties and proms or funerals. I have a few other pins and things you can have if you need them as a matching item, or if you have any friends.

Yours truly,
Scot (your neighbor next door)

sixteen

It was alchemy. Somehow, Sam had distilled the best of the Socratic and chiropractic methods, applied them at the critical moment, permanently straightened Scot's spine, and made a man of him. Scot announced that he and Joey were too old to dress up for Halloween. And he privately confided to me that I shouldn't worry so much about his bed because lots of boys didn't pick up their rooms, and he would try to stay on top of it, "But don't get your hair into a twist if I miss a day here or there, Ed. It's normal for a boy."

It was pathetic and perverse, but I missed my sissy.

Sam urged me to forget the bed for a few weeks so Scot could collect an allowance before the holidays. And I wondered aloud if I was the new sissy in the house. And Sam said, "Maybe just a little prissy on the neatness front. You and Nula have that whole house to yourselves all day, and you both like things exactly the way you like them."

Even the neighbors noticed that there was more strut and less swish about Scot, and his friend Anton took to telephoning every evening. Scot was proud that someone his own age wanted his version of the day's events. Scot also brought home at least one new vulgar word or phrase a day, and he tried it out at dinner, knowing it belonged on the Forbidden List, and that was when Sam started to wonder what he'd done to him, and I didn't make his unmade bed on Wednesday and Thursday evening of the week before Thanksgiving, and then Mildred called before dinner on Friday to tell us that Scot and Tony Burlington had been throwing rocks at the windows of Louisa Bamford's house that afternoon.

This meant Scot had skipped out of ¡Hola!

¿Qué pasa?

Sam stuck Scot on a chair in the kitchen. He stood by the stove and stared at him.

Scot's explanation for the rocks was, "So punish me."

His explanation for skipping Spanish culture class was, "Leave it to Joey to tell on me."

He looked scared, and he was squirming around, trying to get at a bad itch in his pants, but he sounded brave. And for effect, he added, "You're just jealous."

Sam said, "Joey is your friend."

Scot stuck his hand into his pants and scratched as he said, "Well, Ryan's my brother, man. That means Tony is, too."

I felt those words in my spine.

"Okay, man," said Sam. He reached past me and lit the burner under the kettle. "Message received, man. Now it's my turn to give the orders around here, man. First, you go take a bath. And put on clean underwear. And stay in your room until Ed and I come up and talk to you."

Scot stood up, stuck his hands in his pockets, and scratched wildly.

Sam said, "This is serious, Scot."

"I know," Scot said. He was finally starting to look worried. "Is it a disease?"

"I meant the broken window," Sam said. "Just go."

Scot didn't come out of his room for dinner. He did consume a pint of liquid soap and a bottle of antiseptic mouthwash while bathing, and then he put on a turtleneck and socks and no underpants, and he fell asleep on his unmade bed. He looked like his old gooney self. But Sam had painted another picture, and in it, the bald boys had become skinheads, and Scot was throwing stones at Joey Morita, and I lay in bed and hoped that Sam and I were just a couple of sissies ourselves, and we would talk to Joan and Greg and Nula, and we would all remember that we had tossed a few rocks in the wrong direction as kids; and suddenly Scot was screaming, and Sam threw my robe at me, and we ran down the hall and found Scot hopping around naked in his room, scratching his thighs and arms and head, and bleeding all over, and Sam had to holler to be heard, and he told Scot to grab the knobs of his bureau—"Now, Scot! Both hands!"— and he ordered me to get the two-volume *Oxford English Dictionary*, and I had my doubts, but I was scared. Sam yelled, "Don't let go, Scot. Don't let go!" until I returned with the text, from which Sam extracted the handy magnifying glass, which he used to confirm his diagnosis.

He said, "Crabs."

Every inch of my flaky skin was suddenly alive and kicking.

Scot had grown up in Baltimore. He said, "Crabs?" Then he dropped to the floor and sobbed.

Sam ordered me to get him the hydrogen peroxide, to get dressed, and to get to a drugstore.

By the time I found an all-night pharmacy, I'd scratched my own forearms raw, and my face must have looked pretty rugged, too, because the young man at the counter didn't want to touch my money or the three yellow boxes of KILLZ. I waited while he shopped for a pair of rubber gloves.

Scot was standing in the bathtub when I got home. He was wet and shaking. Sam was rubbing his head. They had stopped the bleeding, but the wounds were still foaming with peroxide.

Scot looked at his feet and said, "Please don't tell anyone, Ed. Crabs is a filthy way to go."

Sam asked me to start washing everything in Scot's room. He was reading the directions on the KILLZ box as he said, "Strip the bed—and on my word, Ed, he will make it every day from now on, and he'll make our bed, too, whenever you say so. And Nula's, too."

Scot said, "Is this medicine for delicate skin?"

Sam handed Scot a clean washcloth. "Bite on this."

Scot said, "Why?"

Sam said, "So when you scream, you don't wake Mildred next door."

Scot bit and burbled while Sam poured and rubbed and scraped and rinsed, and finally Scot had to take the washcloth out of his mouth and howl, and Sam sang "The Twelve Days of Christmas," and on the fifth day, Scot joined in, and I stripped the sheets from Scot's bed and added bleach. I went back for everything in his bureau and closet, and before I ruined all of the colored things, Sam told me that it was time in the dryer, not the bleach, that would kill the vermin and their eggs. I changed our sheets and collected everything we'd worn all week, and then Sam carried Scot into his room to sleep.

Sam and I lathered each other up with the pesticide and paved little furrows on each other's chests and backs with

the tiny combs. Sam had seen crabs on clients. I hadn't seen
them for more than twenty years. When I was a junior in
college, I met a soft-spoken guy with violet eyes who lied
about his name, phone number, and marital status, and he
called me Edward, all of which made him seem suave until
the nurse at the infirmary said, "Congratulations. You're the
father of about fifty thousand crabs, and they're all having
babies."

Sam and I had to stay foamy for twenty minutes in the
bathroom.

My arms and neck burned, and then Scot's stoic singing
really impressed me. And Scot had sung more than a Christmas carol. Sam had forced him to spit out the whole sordid
story.

Ryan Burlington, or one of his many girlfriends, was our
crab importer. While Sam and I were out at night with Scot,
and whenever Ryan felt like skipping school, he let himself
into our house with Scot's key, and he serviced his harem in
Scot's bed. This was why Ryan was so religious about his
Sunday visits. Scot's sermons included advance details
about vacancies in the flophouse. And Scot collected five
bucks from Ryan most Sundays, which kept him in bubble
bath.

Sam said, "I'm actually grateful to the crabs. Without
them, the story is so pathetic we might want to pity the kid."

Tony, the younger brother, hadn't really provided any of
the promised protection, though Scot had invoked his name
and found it effective with fifth-graders. But it was Tony who
had dared and taunted Scot to break a window in the house
next door, and Sam said Scot seemed to realize it was mostly
designed to make Scot look bad in front of Ryan and one of
his girlfriends, who were sitting on the stoop. Scot figured

he'd thrown "around twenty-seven" rocks before he managed to break a bedroom window, and then Ryan told him to knock it off and punched Tony in the head.

The bubbling foam was almost absorbed. I said, "So I've basically been Ryan Burlington's chambermaid?"

Sam said, "And Scot's been collecting your tips."

In the morning, Sam marched Scot across the street with a yellow box in his hand. Ryan answered the door, and he immediately apologized and grabbed the KILLZ and asked Sam where he could get more, and then he asked us not to say anything to Tom, his stepfather, who was by then standing behind the storm door. Tom came out, and then he yelled for Tony, who had been spying from the bathroom with the window open. Tony joined us on their front lawn, and then Andrea appeared in the window, unmasked.

Tom said, "The next time you see these two, you won't recognize them." He belted Tony in the gut and doubled him over, and then Tony hobbled into the house, and Andrea yelled, "Call your father. Tell him to get over here before Tom gets to your brother," and she shut the window.

Tom said, "She knows I won't hurt anybody," but we all knew he would. Eager for an ally, he said, "Hey, Sam, why don't I split the cost of the window with you?"

Sam turned to Scot, who said, "That's part of my punishment. I have to clean up my own messes from now on."

Ryan looked genuinely pained when he said, "I shouldn't have made you do it, Scot. I fucked up, man." He tried to touch Scot's arm, but Scot was too mindful of the crabs to tolerate contact.

Scot said, "I'm a boy, Ryan. We're all just boys." Scot backed up a few steps, and then he added, "You're not invited over anymore."

As Sam and I followed Scot up our front steps, Ryan took a blow to the back of his head that knocked him down, and it wasn't long before the boys' first father showed up and loaded two suitcases and some brown bags into the trunk of his car, and when Andrea stood on her stoop, she was wearing her mask, and one of her husbands yelled, "You married him," and it was weeks before anyone saw either of the Burlington boys again.

Scot watched it all from his bed, which was draped in a sheet, as were two sofas in the living room, where Sam and I sat until we were prepared to take the cure a second time to kill any eggs we were incubating for the crabs.

Sam said, "Boarding school?"

I said, "Nunnery."

I stood up. It was time to talk to the prisoner.

Sam plucked a corner of the sheet on his sofa and held it up. He said, "It doesn't even look like our living room anymore."

But it did from where I stood. "It's ours, all right. Big table. Four sofas. Upholstery by Scot."

When I entered his bedroom, Scot was sitting cross-legged, and his head was in his hands. I said, "What are you thinking about it all?"

He looked sober, sobered. The binge with the Burlington boys had taken its toll. His gaze was sad and steady, and his skin was pretty scraped up.

Innocence is a windfall. We trade it. We spend it. We squander it. We can never earn a penny of it back.

Scot looked a little poorer, but he hadn't cleaned out his account. When I knelt by his bed, he burst into tears and said, "Oh, Ed. How am I ever going to explain this to Mildred?"

seventeen

In New England, Thanksgiving is the day we celebrate the cold, wet weather, the dark afternoons, and the miseries of indoor life. If we didn't stuff turkeys and grind up cranberries, we'd have to stuff socks into each other's mouths and grind our teeth more. As we did every year, Sam and I went to Joan and Greg's the night before Thanksgiving and stayed up too late making pies for the poor and drinking some of Greg's holiday bonus. Upstairs, Hank slept, and Scot sat on the floor by his bed watching television, or so we hoped. It was Scot's first real break since he'd broken the window in Louisa Bamford's house. After he and Sam had contacted Louisa's family and made the repairs, Scot had been straightening up piles of old junk and washing shelves in corners of our basement that even he hadn't explored, and he'd also been on loan to Mildred and George for an hour a day—a community-service program Sam had devised to teach Scot that he was a force in other people's lives, whether he was disturbing their peace or lugging boxes of Christmas decorations down from their spider-infested attics.

Scot's love for Mildred trumped his vertigo—"She and the Georges don't even fit through the trapdoor in the ceiling anymore," he explained—and he was treating his arachnophobia chemically. He'd gone through two bottles of bug repellent in four days, and because he couldn't sleep with his smelly self, he'd plugged lavender air fresheners into the electrical sockets in his bedroom.

Sam complained that he couldn't taste his tea. Nula searched my coat pockets at work and accused me of hiding a sachet. "My cigarettes taste like something Martha Stewart invented," she said, and she sent me home with two bottles of liquid peppermint soap, for which Scot happily traded the plug-ins.

We were becoming expert at treating his symptoms, as if we all knew we were managing an incurable disease.

Name the disease.

Joan and Sam were rolling and cutting crusts. Greg and I were in charge of fillings. There were two wall ovens and a freestanding convection box, and three varieties of cognac, courtesy of the partners at Greg's firm. We were all feeling tired and tipsy, except Joan, who was abstaining because she was pregnant, and "nine months is bad enough, but if I start serving cocktails the kid will never want to come out."

It had not been an easy autumn, and we wanted to put everything into a hot oven, bake it, and tell each other how good it was. But we could barely swallow it all, and there was still that freshly killed twenty-two pound turkey in our refrigerator at home, as well as Sam's ten-pound lump of flavored tofu and tempeh, which looked like a New Age egg laid by the New World bird, and most of our friends were busy stuffing mushrooms and candying yams for the annual drop-in feast on Finn Street.

And no one knew that Scot had Super-Computed invitations to Joey, Anton, and Carla, as well as their many relatives, to "drop by for holiday cheer and some other dessert around seven," which was about the time Nula traditionally asked Sam to go outside with her and check something under the hood of her car, where she would meet him with the necessary tools—a couple of fat joints purchased from the teenage vendors at the Harvard Square subway kiosk. Nula said it was pure patriotism; once a year, she made sure Sam hadn't turned into a Puritan.

As she completed a particularly handsome lattice top for a bumbleberry pie, Joan said, "This is a work of art. I should quit my job."

And Greg said, "Then you'd be stuck at home with the kids," and it was clear he hadn't meant to say it out loud. It was an electrical discharge, a late bolt of lightning from a storm that had thundered through the house sometime before we got there, and it shocked us all for a second, suspending activity until Joan dipped a pastry brush into a bowl of milk and dampened her woven strips of dough, and Sam added a few drops of ice water to his dry ingredients, and that was our cue to get back to work, but Greg didn't stir.

I poured myself a few inches of a new, bitter cognac, and instead of stoking the stove in my belly like the smoother stuff did, this dose headed right to the back of my throat, where it began to burn out my tonsils.

Joan rolled together a few scraps of dough and punched out tiny pastry stars.

She worked as a commercial real-estate agent, and she always made her job sound mesmerizingly dull. Greg made plenty of money, and their tenant paid the better part of their mortgage, and the day care and nanny costs for two kids would nearly equal Joan's yearly commissions. She wasn't going to quit.

Some things you can talk about, and some things you can't. Right?

I said, "Are you ever afraid that when your kids are eleven, you won't know much more about them than we know about Scot?"

Joan looked stung, but she smiled when she said, "Sure, when you put it that way, I get the willies."

Sam said, "Are you drunk, Ed?"

Something thudded to the floor above us, but then we heard a few tentative footfalls on the floorboards in Hank's room; whoever had hit the deck was not dead.

Joan was looking up when she said, "You only want to know so much about your kids."

I said, "But you want to be sure your kids don't turn out like Scot, right?" I wanted someone to say it aloud. Scot was an unfit child. I was an unfit father. Had no one else noticed? The experiment was not going well, and every time Sam cracked Scot's back, some new and amazing innate intelligence was released, and then Scot got another bright idea, and we found him applying a depilatory cream to his underarms.

Name the disease.

Another thud.

Greg chopped up some apples he'd already chopped up.

Sam said, "Let's not talk about the kids."

Greg said, "Why would Hank turn into Scot?"

I poured myself another tonsillectomy and said, "Why would Scot turn into Scot?"

Greg said, "Maybe we should have just bought some pies this year."

Sam said, "Or put Ed in a shelter."

Greg stuck the squeaky cork into the cognac bottle.

Joan said, "Well, don't shut him off now, Greg. He's got both feet in his mouth, and he's gonna need something to wash them down." She held up her shiny patchwork pie, showed it off to each of us, and then she slid it into the convection oven, unplugged the bottle, and topped off my glass.

Sam said, "You're going to regret this in the morning, Ed."

Joan said, "Get pregnant, Sam. Then you'll know about morning regrets." She poured herself more ginger ale and clinked her glass against mine. "Listen to me, Ed. I don't know how he did it, but Sam got you pregnant. Scot is your kid." She put her arm around my shoulder and raised her glass. "To Scot," she yelled.

Greg gamely added, "And to Sam and Ed, for a job well done."

Sam said, "Hear, hear," as he slapped the rolling pin down against another ball of dough, which looked a lot like my head.

Another thud.

Sam stopped and stared at me. "Is it safe to ask what Scot is doing up there?"

I said, "I doubt it."

Greg said, "No harm done."

Another thud.

Greg said, "Hank jumps around up there. I'll worry about it when the plaster cracks."

It was cracking. We just couldn't see it yet. I said, "I'll go up."

Greg said, "I'll go up with you, Ed."

Before I left the kitchen, I drained the full glass of cognac, because unlike Joan and Greg, and maybe even unlike Sam, I was no longer expecting a normal child.

Greg patted me on the back before we entered the dim bedroom. I think he really believed we might find the boys playing Cowboys and Indians or building a go-cart.

Hank was lying on the far side of his bed, and though the only light in the room was the flashing television screen, you could see he had on a bath-towel skirt and some of his hair was rubber-banded into a little fountain of a ponytail. Both boys were wearing tee shirts, which were hiked up and knotted above their midriffs. Scot was stuck about halfway down into an unsuccessful performance of the splits. He'd either rolled up the cuffs of his trousers, or just ditched the pants, but above his white socks, there was a stretch of bare skin, and then something that looked like yellow leggings and a puffy yellow skirt, and I remembered that he had started out the evening in a new yellow V-neck sweater.

Scot froze.

Hank was asleep, or old enough to know how to fake it.

Greg was like a kid in a museum. He kept looking, but it wasn't sinking in.

I whispered, "Cheerleading."

After that, Greg didn't want to look at me, and that's why it's helpful to have televisions scattered around the house. The boys had been watching a football game. Greg sat on the edge of Hank's bed. He was hoping to capitalize on the sports theme, I think. He said, "This isn't a bowl game already, is it?"

Scot said, "I've never heard of the bowl game. This one is just called regular football, I think."

Greg said, "Oh."

Scot retracted his legs and gathered himself into a crouch. He couldn't tell yet if he was supposed to be ashamed or not. He wrapped his arms around his knees, so he was ready to weep or to explode into a big spread-eagle jump.

From his post on the bed, Greg pointed at Scot's hands.

Scot was holding several pairs of Hank's socks.

I whispered, "Pom-poms."

Greg stood up, and I really thought he might walk right out of the room, but he said, "Do you want to be a cheerleader, Scot? Do you wish you were a cheerleader?"

I couldn't tell if the question was benign or vindictive.

Scot knew he was just a bedroom cheerleader, and he was appropriately humble. "The cheerleaders on TV are professionals, Mr. Koester. You can't just say you want to be one of them. You have to invent a whole new routine and be able to do it perfectly in time for the judges."

If Scot had been talking about football, Greg would have listened with genuine amused interest to Scot's attempts to make sense of the game, taught him some of the standard lingo, helped him to appreciate the finer points, asked him an easy question or two—Do you think they'll pass? Has the defense played well today?—and told him he ought to come by and toss a football around before the game next Sunday. But that give and take, that backyard teaching and learning of simple social skills and self-confidence and respect, that casual way many honorable men have been made—it was never going to happen. I didn't think football was noble, but neither was cheerleading. And Greg was one of the good guys. And Sam and I were running out of friends.

I turned off the television, and Scot didn't protest. Very quietly—so maybe Hank really was asleep—Scot said, "Can you do the splits, Mr. Koester?"

Greg said, "No, I don't think so. Most men can't."

Scot said, "Did you ever try?"

Greg said, "No, not for a long time."

Scot said, "But you tried? At least once or something?"

Greg said, "Yes, once maybe."

It was dark. They were whispering. This gave Scot the home-field advantage.

Scot said, "Were you alone when you practiced?"

Greg said, "It was so long ago, I don't really remember it, Scot."

Scot said, "Did you ever want to be a cheerleader, Mr. Koester?"

Greg said, "No, never."

Scot said, "Never? Not even for a minute?"

Greg said, "No."

Scot said, "Really?"

Greg said, "Really."

Scot said, "If you ever try again, do it in the bathroom and put a washcloth under each foot. That way you slide. And stick your hands up in the air over your head for gravity. If you have a friend to help you, or Mrs. Koester, she can grab your hands and push down, to put extra pressure on you."

Greg let a few seconds pass before he said, "From now on, even if Hank asks for it, I don't want you to dress him up like a girl, Scot. It's not okay." He was embarrassed.

Scot said, "I'm sorry, Mr. Koester." He dropped his pom-poms.

I said, "We really have to get home, Scot. Go pull yourself together. I'll meet you downstairs."

There was light in the hall, and Scot's skirt drooped down around his ankles as he closed the bathroom door. I was still half in Hank's room. Greg patted me on the back again and said, "Maybe Scot is too old to be playing with Hank so much. It's not his fault, really." It really wasn't. Greg removed Hank's skirt and ponytail, tucked him in, and hovered over the bed like a doctor with a critically ill patient. I watched him touch his son's head with the back of his hand, gauging the testosterone level, perhaps.

In the kitchen, Sam and Joan were making fast work of pies that were supposed to provide us with slow, homemade fun. I tried to deliver my report on the scene upstairs as Joan always talked about her job. I wanted it to sound boring, but the bare midriffs worked against me.

Joan said, "Why would he want to be a cheerleader?"

I said, "Team spirit?"

Sam said, "I don't even understand why cheerleaders want to be cheerleaders."

I said, "That'll make it hard to understand Scot."

Sam sounded defeated when he said, "The socks in his hands and the little fake skirts. Why is he so hung up on costumes?"

Joan said, "That sweater thing was . . . elaborate."

I said, "It wasn't a costume, exactly. It was his uniform." Unlike Joan and Sam, I'd coveted a pom-pom in the past. Name the disease. "He knows we won't buy him a pleated skirt and megaphone, so he has to improvise. Maybe it's our fault. If we saw him hitting rocks with a stick, we'd buy him a proper baseball and an aluminum bat." And I might have stopped right there, but Greg returned looking shell-shocked, looking for sympathy, I think, and I didn't want to hear about how hard it was to understand Scot, or to explain Scot, or to tolerate Scot, so I said, "I really don't mind if he wants to be a cheerleader a couple of hours a week. Plenty of people spend whole weekends cheering for their favorite teams. The Cowboys. The Buccaneers. The Bears. Really, the Bears. And then the quarterback drops into the pocket and they pop right out of their chairs and it's in the air and—oh, god, a perfect spiral—and they can see he's going for the end zone and they can't help screaming while the ball is in the air—Go! Go! Go!—and the ball is still in the air and the wide receiver is two steps ahead of the defender and—Catch it! Catch the damn thing!—and they're stomping their feet and the receiver's hands are up and it's . . . it's . . . Yes! Yes! Touchdown! And then? And then?" And then I did the funky chicken dance, the dorky end-zone celebration performed each week by America's manliest men and their admirers in homes all across the country.

When I was done, I said, "If Scot did that in public, he'd be hanged."

Sam said, "What makes you think you're safe?"

Greg said, "Probably my cognac."

And then I think we all wished I would disappear into the sidelines, but Scot was still upstairs in the bathroom, probably trying on the Koesters' shower caps.

Finally, Joan said, "Or we could talk about the guest list. Is anyone we don't know going to be there tomorrow?"

Sam said, "Ed."

I said, "Ed? That asshole? Please don't give him anything to drink."

Greg said, "Oh, forget it, Ed. Forget it. Maybe somebody should take a look at the mince pies. Isn't something burning?"

And something was burning—maybe a pie, maybe a bridge. It was hard to tell just then. But the team of Joan and Sam was back in action, and I rinsed out the dishes stacked up in the sink, and Greg opened each oven several times, and he glanced hopefully at the stairs, but nothing was happening fast enough for him. He wanted the evening to end. Forget it. Forget it. Scot and I had both gone too far, shown a bit too much skin. I felt bad, as if I was to blame—principally, I think, because I was to blame. It wasn't a big drama, and it had a relatively happy ending, but for many years, we had all enjoyed a friendship that did not include domestic theater. Since Scot's arrival, we'd spent more and more time together, and we were all overhearing a lot of each other's backstage chatter and seeing more than the audience is supposed to see. And with the football speech, I had dropped the script entirely, and now we would all have to improvise our next few scenes together.

No one had said so until tonight, but we all knew that Scot and Hank were not natural playmates, and neither were Greg and I. Sam and Joan were working on a lifelong friendship. They were both businesspeople in Harvard Square, and they referred clients to each other, which made it more fun to gossip about the worst of them. And three or four times a week, while Sam and Joan were trotting on neighboring treadmills at a health club in a Harvard Square hotel, Greg was playing basketball with other bankers, and I was on the phone with Nula trying to finish the Sunday crossword puzzle.

Scot got as far as the bottom of the stairs, where he'd left his coat and hat, and he couldn't come any closer. I waved good-bye to the pies, and it wasn't until we were safe in his bedroom that Scot said, "I think Mr. Koester is afraid I'm infecting Hank."

I said, "With what?" I thought he was referring to the crabs, and that was enough to make me feel there was some extracurricular activity on the skin behind my ears.

But Scot said, "You know, with my cooties."

Cooties: the enduring grade-school diagnosis of the disease carried by the fat, the femmey, the dark, the newly breasted, the inappropriately erect, the poorly dressed, the too-tall, the grossly stupid, and the annoyingly smart. Standard treatments: harassment and isolation.

I said, "Mr. Koester doesn't think you have cooties, Scot." But I was faking it. Greg wanted his boy to be a real boy, and Scot wasn't apt to wrestle with Hank or to refuse him a baby bonnet if he wanted one.

Scot tried and failed to squeeze his feet into his favorite old slippered brown pajamas, which he'd pulled from a shelf in his closet. They were too small. He was bigger than he was when he arrived. Somewhere, he had two other pairs of pajamas and a nightshirt, but he settled for the top of the old brown ones and a pair of underpants, and then he slipped under his blanket. "Did people ever hate you when you were just a gay boy, Ed?"

"When I was your age?"

"Yes," said Scot, but he scooted out of bed and held up his hand. "Hold it. Forgot to brush." He ran down the hall.

I should have followed him and splashed some cold water on my face.

Scot came rushing back, looking rabid, and I said, "Forgot to rinse," and he sprinted to the bathroom and then back to his bed.

I said, "Most people didn't know I was gay until I was in college, Scot."

He sat up. "Did you know?"

I said, "I did."

He said, "So you faked it?" Clearly, it had never occurred to him that not wearing his earrings might be a costume, too.

"Sometimes," I said. "Sometimes I wanted to be just like the other kids, so I acted like I was. And sometimes, I just wasn't gay in the way they thought of being gay, and that was enough to fool them, I guess."

Scot said, "Ed? Suppose I'm not gay?"

I said, "That's cool. Why?" It was true. I didn't care, but that seemed lazy of me. Was it my responsibility to have a preference about his preferences? Could he figure out his orientation if I didn't offer a clear sense of direction?

Scot said, "I don't know if I'm gay, or maybe I'm just faking everybody out."

I said, "Do you ever fake it?" I think I meant, Who are you? For eleven years, he had lived as the child of a sweet, sad junkie whose maternal instinct had turned suicidal. His father had waived his rights to see him before he was born. His other blood relatives had also waved him off. He was the ward of the brother of one of his mother's boyfriends. Everyone around him was faking it. All he had to show for himself was his authentically red hair, which was not really a big help. I had devoted hours to thinking about what Scot wore, how he walked, and what he might do next. I had discussed the effect Scot had on me and on Sam and on other people. But Scot was a stranger, a black hole, a cast-off pair of pajamas. Whoever he was, whoever he might have been, I realized it wasn't going to be so easy for him to cast off Greg Koester's disapproval, or the oddity of having gay guardians instead of regular parents, or the memory of being tripped while he carried his tray in the cafeteria. It made me morose. I hated the world—all of us, except maybe Mildred Monterosso, who was such a good faker that she made everyone believe she liked everyone but not quite as much as she liked you.

Scot said, "When you were a boy, did you enjoy gym class?"

I said, "I always liked gym class."

Scot said, "Liked it, liked it? Or fake liked it?"

"Liked it, liked it," I said. In fact, I loved it because my physical skills were better than average, and this meant either I wasn't gay or nobody I knew really knew what it meant to be gay, and I seemed to win either way. And then there was the trampoline. I loved the trampoline more than I loved art class and those Biblical movies in which the men wore steel skirts and let their hair grow long. I was a good flipper and an excellent twister, and it was deeply rewarding to have the coach—a sturdy young man in a sweatsuit— stand around with his hands in the air, "spotting" me. And then he'd praise me enthusiastically for my skill—which basically consisted of pointing my toes and hopping around like a cheerleader, tricks I had perfected in the backyard when I hoped the neighbors weren't watching.

As eleven-year-olds, Scot and I were both symptomatic.

Prescribe a treatment.

Name the disease.

Be careful, doctor. Before you cut out someone's heart, you should know that I practiced "Swing it to the left, Swing it to the right" and touching my toes in the air because I admired the boys on the field. I had not figured out how to choreograph my desires. I wanted to be wanted like a cheerleader. But I think Scot was straining his groin muscles and singing "When the Saints Go Marching In" because he admired the girls. More than any football player, and thus perhaps more than any cheerleader, Scot really dug the way their hair flounced right back into place after a handspring. He knew that eyeliner haphazardly applied could blind you, and he was indignant when he found out that it wasn't cool for girls to show some stubble.

Joan was right. Scot's imitations were elaborate. It was elaborate to be a girl.

Would he always imitate them? Was it up to me to teach him a more insincere form of flattery?

I did not become a cheerleader. I played hockey in high school, because I did not rely on my stick for balance, and that was the cut for the team. In western New York State in the seventies, the unendowed day schools and Catholic academies fielded ice hockey teams because it was hard to attract male teachers for $10, 000 a year, even when you threw in the title of yearbook advisor. Halperin Day operated as a farm team for the Division One public school coaching staffs. Handsome young men with Phys. Ed. and psychology degrees taught us what handsome young men have always known about algebra, marine sciences, and world history: The answers are in the back of the book. They skipped afternoon classes to attend college and pro games in Buffalo and Toronto, courted local sports reporters, and turned a generation of unpromising young athletes into high-sticking, low-blow specialists. Winning was everything for these transient coaches, and they didn't care how many kids got hurt while they worked their way up to jobs in the big-city schools. This made them heroes among our parents, who did not have the leeway to swat us with snow shovels or body-check us into the walls at home. Our fathers and mothers cheered whenever anybody's son was slammed into the boards. Bleeding was also a crowd pleaser, but the big moment always involved a kid on his back on the ice. It usually took the players a few minutes to notice him, which gives you some indication of our ability to spot the puck and handle a pass, but eventually we'd respond to the crowd's silence. If Tim Grogan was in goal, he'd yell, "We've got a floater."

It always occurred to us that the downed player might be dead. Beneath our plastic helmets and puffy pads and straps, we were boys, and we rarely knew when we'd gone too far until the car was screeching toward a telephone pole or someone was prone and pale. Usually, the floater was just unconscious or too scared to stand up. We'd circle him and poke him with our sticks, the way our fathers investigated road kill. Then a coach or a team trainer would slide out in his shoes and try to get a pulse, and when the kid talked, this was taken as proof that his back was not broken, and he was hauled off the ice. The fans on both sides loved this part, especially if his arms were slung around the shoulders of at least one player from the opposing team.

Symptomatic of what?

Name that disease.

I hadn't seen Scot skate yet, but I doubted he would take to the sport. He looked like a floater. Maybe he would end up in white slacks and a letter sweater, one of the well-groomed, smiling boys who stand at the bottom of the pyramid of girls, supporting their idols. Living with Sam, he'd have the back for it.

My adult life has offered me precious few opportunities to cash in on my ice time, though I'm a good person to follow onto a crowded subway.

But cheerleading practice was not wasted on me. It's what I do for a living. I stand on the sidelines, whipping up enthusiasm for the masters.

Who do you love?

Bernini.

Louder.

BERNINI.

Scot was not asleep. "Ed? Some things you can talk about, and some things you can't, right?"

Was that right? What was the lesson of the pies? Or was that the Social Contract?

"Ed?"

"Yes?"

"How many people were on the *Mayflower*?"

I said, "I don't know. Two or three hundred. Why?"

Scot said, "One hundred and two."

I said, "Is that what you were studying in school this week?"

Scot said, "I looked it up on the Web. Do you know what most of them were called?"

Somehow I doubted I did, but I was game. "Pilgrims?"

Scot said, "Thirty-five of them."

I said, "What were the rest of them called?" His eyes were closed, and I didn't know if he was asleep or unsure of the answer. I said, "Maybe they were called Pilgrims, too?"

It was my best guess. My sophomore history teacher had called them "the buckle-headed sons of bitches who wouldn't give you or your friends an inch if it wasn't called for in the King James Bible." Her name was Pauline Schoop. She taught at Halperin Day for two years, and she spent both of her Christmas vacations in jail because she and the four other practicing atheists in suburban Buffalo insisted on sleeping among the plastic farm animals in the town-sponsored manger. My father liked to say, "That's what happens to people with strong convictions," to which my mother would add, "Only if they act on them," and as I sat on the edge of Scot's bed with his old pajamas in my hands, I knew they were right. They typically were. My parents described the world and its ways pretty accurately to my sister and me, and because they didn't think the world was broken, they didn't waste any time teaching either of us how to fix it. When Pauline Schoop was fired and I hotly defended her controversial theory of history, my father said, "You can waste your whole life being right, son. She may be a genius for all I know, but she's a fanatic." My mother agreed. She said, "Most people are content to be part of the carpet, Eddie. We're all just the little threads that go into the big picture. Your Miss Schoop is part of the lunatic fringe. Nobody is saying she can't stay out there, but no normal person can live in a house with wall-to-wall fringe. It isn't practical."

Scot said, "Are you okay, Ed?" He was almost asleep.

I said, "I'm okay, Scot. I was just thinking."

Scot said, "Me, too." His eyes were shut. His breathing was slow and rhythmic, like any one of us at rest. We all need our rest. My father taught me that. Whenever I tried to unsettle him with a startling new plan for my future—Architecture! Theatrical design! House painting!—he'd say, "It's fine with me, son, as long as you can sleep through the night."

I stood up. Scot didn't respond to my movement until I was almost out the door. He didn't open his eyes. He said, "There were only thirty-five Pilgrims. That leaves sixty-seven who weren't. In America, that's called a majority. But the Pilgrims called them the Strangers. Those are the ones who were probably our forefathers, right?"

I said, "The Strangers?" Maybe this was the lesson of the pies.

"Yeah," said Scot. "They were like us, right?"

I figured I could nail this one, but I had missed every other question on this history quiz, so I demurred. "Like us how?"

Scot said, "They were atheists. Like you and Sam and me. They didn't believe in God."

Missed it by a mile. I said, "We'll discuss it in the morning."

Scot said, "Ed?"

Would the night never end?

"Yes, Scot?"

Scot said, "If Mr. Koester never wanted to be a cheerleader, how come he was practicing his splits?"

eighteen

When Sam came to bed, I was reading the story of the *May-flower* in the one-volume *Columbia Encyclopedia* with the magnifying glass from the two-volume *OED*.

Sam said, "Are the crabs back?"

We were all still jumpy.

"No," I said, "It's a story about Strangers in Capes," and I gave him a synopsis of Scot's research, with an emphasis on our status as atheists. I didn't mention Miss Schoop.

Sam said, "He's right. I don't worship a god. You didn't listen to the telephone message, did you?"

"No," I said. "But what about me and God?"

Sam said, "That's between you and God."

I said, "What about me and God and Scot?"

Sam said, "That's between you and God, too."

His feet were cold. Mine were warm. This occasioned an impromptu and vigorous heat-transfer operation, but that's between Sam and me.

Afterward, Sam said, "Well."

I said, "Well?"

He said, "Apology accepted."

"Thanks," I said.

Sam said, "It was Billy. On the machine."

I said, "What does he want?"

Sam said, "He was calling from D.C."

I said, "What does he want?"

Sam said, "He's engaged."

I said, "What does he want?"

Sam said, "He wants to bring her by tomorrow."

I said, "He won't come."

Sam said, "They're going to live in D. C. or Baltimore."

I said, "He won't come."

Sam said, "I know."

I said, "I don't think this is just between you and Billy. I don't think he should come."

Sam said, "I know."

I said, "What do you think?"

"I don't know," Sam said. "He's my brother. He didn't leave a number."

God. Billy. A fiancée, who probably came with kids. We didn't have enough dinner plates.

nineteen

I woke to the smell of cinnamon toast. Or pecan rolls. Or a Sugar 'n' Spice bath candle. In our house, you never knew. Sam was not in bed. I followed my nose to the spare room. Sam was sitting on the floor, between the StairMaster and the futon, in the half-lotus. A clay pot of incense was smoking beside him. This was serious. This was beyond chiropractic and kasha. This was the atom bomb in Sam's spiritual arsenal. His eyes were half-open, which I'd always thought was a trick used by meditators to keep themselves awake, but Sam said he did it because the whole point of meditating was to see something that was only half-there.

Something like Billy.

Scot was eating cereal in the kitchen. He was wearing his yellow sweater, rightside up, and the bottoms of his old brown pajamas, which sort of fit now that he'd cut the feet off. He was reading the newspaper. He said, "Sam made special tea for your headache. In the black pot. Is the president a vegetarian?"

I didn't know where to start. I made coffee. I said, "I don't think so."

Scot said, "There's a picture of him with a turkey he's not eating."

I said, "The president does that every year. He saves one turkey."

Scot said, "Just one?"

"Just one," I said. "It's a tradition."

Scot read the rest of the story, which gave me time to drink two cups of coffee and pour half a cup of tea down the drain.

When Scot pushed the front section my way, he said, "You were right. The president and his family do eat turkeys. This one is just a fake."

Suddenly, I needed that tea. I poured myself a cup—for real. It tasted like cinnamon.

Scot flipped though the other sections until he found the comics.

I put our turkey into a roasting pan on the counter.

Scot said, "The Strangers weren't all atheists, Ed. A lot of them were regular Protestants. We have to be careful about specific generalizations."

I guessed I was getting the remnants of a sermon Sam had delivered earlier. I nodded reverently and chopped onions.

Scot said, "If we want to, Sam will teach us how to just sit there and clear our brains out with him. It's ancient, but you can leave the room if you get cramps."

I piled the ingredients for stuffing on the table, and Scot instinctively peeled off the shrink-wrap and looked for brown spots and wilted leaves, and when I told him that I believed we were all pilgrims on a journey, he said, "Do you think it should be sit-down or buffet-style today?"

Sometimes Scot was a radio, and someone else was spinning his dial.

I opted for the buffet and showed Scot how to position his knuckles so he could chop the celery without chopping off his fingers, and he said it was just like feeding carrots to a horse, as if he and Julie had kept a couple of old nags in the brownstone in Baltimore. I sautéed sausage and onions, and then Scot tossed in his contribution, and he thought I was joking when I told him to add rosemary, thyme, and sage in pinches until he tried it, and then he popped open the bag of bread crumbs and poured what hadn't spilled to the floor into the pot, and then I told him he had to take over, so he stood on a chair and used both hands to stir it all up each time I added more fresh apple cider, which we stopped to sip and spill from the bottle several times, until we were both satisfied with the mess we had made.

I said he should take a break while I mopped up, so he sat beside the turkey on the counter, and I dumped the butt ends of onions and celery into the sink and swept crumbs into a postcard I kept on a shelf instead of buying a dustpan. There were a lot of peelings and droppings, and Scot nodded whenever he thought it was time to flip on the disposal switch, and I nodded when I agreed, and then he put his hand on the turkey and said, "The Koesters have to go to Connecticut today."

I said, "Did Sam speak to them?" Were they avoiding us?

Scot nodded. "Mr. Koester's mother is taking a stroke like every hour or so, and she isn't young, either. If you know what I mean."

I said, "I know she's been pretty sick. I'll miss them, though."

Scot nodded. He opened the silverware drawer with his bare feet and used it as a footrest. It's the sort of innovation I admire. He didn't put his feet on the forks; he kept them balanced on the sides. He was trying to adjust the raggedy cuffs of his pajamas, which were riding up toward his knees. Without the feet, the pajamas really didn't work. He said, "Billy might come, and he might not come. We can't rely on it."

I hated being the last one up in the morning. It was like being late for a movie.

I said, "Are you okay with that?"

Scot looked directly at me and said, "He's not *my* brother."

I said, "I just wondered if you liked the idea."

Scot said, "Which idea?"

I said, "Billy."

Scot shrugged. He petted the turkey a few times, as if it were a cat. "I wish Julie could come home."

Billy and Julie.

"Then if she wanted to stay overnight, we have the spare room, plus I'm on vacation for a couple days." He shook his head. No. No. No. No. He wasn't going to cry. Why not?

I didn't want to cry if Scot didn't want to cry, though our mute camaraderie wasn't very noble; it was more like peer pressure.

Scot said, "Everybody we know knows she killed herself, right?"

I said, "No."

Scot opened his mouth, but he didn't speak. He closed the silverware drawer with his legs and paddled his feet like flippers. I think he wanted to say something mean or dismissive, call me a stupid liar, maybe, or accuse me of faking it. He didn't though.

He wasn't a cruel kid. In this way, Scot was a bad investment. He rarely paid out a fair return on the insults and injuries he collected. What would he do with them all?

Predict his future.

In the future, he would stick a needle in his arm.

In the future, he would stick around and help his friend Carla clean up her mess when she didn't make it to the bathroom.

In the future, he would sit in Robert's office with a shopping bag of unhappy memories, and though it would be too late to return the assorted ill-fitting and embarrassing items a boy like Scot collects over the years, it might not be too late to learn how to be less receptive, more selective.

In the future, he would meditate on his misfortunes and transcend them.

In the future, he would lop off his penis and take pills to make his breasts grow.

In the future, he would remember the lesson of the bald boys—compromise: Crabs won't kill you, but Tony Burlington ordered weapons from the back of magazines.

In the future, he would have to decide for himself whether Julie's death was accidental or intentional.

I didn't know.

I didn't know if daredevils wanted to die or wanted to live. Or soldiers. Or martyrs. Or even smokers, or the little girls who stand at the very top of the pyramid.

What did I know?

I knew that vertigo was unreasonable, but I also knew the unreasoning impulse that rose in me whenever I got to the edge of a cliff. I was not afraid of falling. I was afraid I might jump. That was not a reason not to climb to the top, but it was a reason to take Sam along.

I said, "I don't know what happened to Julie, Scot. I don't suppose I ever will. I just want to do everything I can to make sure it doesn't happen to you or Sam."

Scot scratched the crown of his head and very softly, to the turkey, he said, "That makes me happy, and it makes me sad." Then, in a wavering, wiry voice that threatened to snap at any moment, Scot said, "Do you mind if I use one of our good pens?"

I said, "In the other drawer, next to the silverware."

He opened it with his feet. "Pick a number," he said. He chose a red felt-tip marker, which he tested on his palm. "Between one and thirty, or thirty-one."

I was game. I said, "Eleven."

Scot smiled. "That's how old I am."

"I know," I said. "Lucky number."

He nodded, then he closed the drawer with one foot and hopped down off the counter. He said, "This was invented for when you're unhappy, or when we were really worried about something, like the car getting towed again." He flipped the calendar forward to December and made an X in the box of the eleventh day. "Now, we just don't think about it until the time comes, okay?"

I said, "Okay. Does it work?"

Scot said, "Usually you forget."

It made sense. Julie had run out of unmarked boxes on her calendar. I said, "Showers before we stop by Mildred's?"

Scot nodded. On his way out of the kitchen, he said, "There's something in a basket on the front porch for you."

Moses, probably.

twenty

In the basket, nestled safely among many new white socks, was the bumbleberry pie. There was a note.

"Blessed are the pie makers, for they shall be friends."

twenty-one

At three o'clock, the living room lights flashed on and off a few times, and everything stopped. Just like that. We all went still and silent for a second, and then for a few seconds more, and then someone said, "Thanksgiving is a dangerous day."

Billy had arrived.

He walked into the crowded living room, picked up somebody else's glass of red wine, and smiled at several people he didn't know, like a celebrity. He was wearing a black suit with narrow lapels and pegged cuffs, and a thin black tie. He'd added a mustache and goatee to his repertoire, but he hadn't brought the fiancée, unless she'd been told to wait in the car while he warmed up the crowd.

Nula found me near the entrance to the kitchen and tugged on my arm.

I nodded.

She said, "I may have to borrow some of Scot's perfume."

Scot was leaning against Sam by the fireplace, where Robert and Danny and Sam's attorney Barbara and her partner, Donna, had spent most of the afternoon rearranging logs and kindling and producing one fire after another that burned about as long as a good match.

Billy bowed deeply to Sam.

Behind Billy, Sam's partner, Jeremy, was standing on the stairs and counting heads again. Every time someone new walked in, Jeremy counted again, as if people were sneaking friends in under their coats and hats. Jeremy was desperately trying to convince Sam that we didn't have enough food, because he had a friend who owned a chain of seafood restaurants, and Jeremy wanted to make the call—"I just have to make one call, Sam. Even on a holiday. One call."—that would set in motion a chain of events that would eventually land a man in a van on Finn Street with twenty pounds of cooked shrimp and "as much smoked salmon as you can stand–you'll have it for days with eggs, bagels, and the capers—I can't begin to describe the quality of the capers. Like grapes." Jeremy waved wildly for a moment, and then I spotted his wife, Clare, a small, fit woman who carried Jeremy's cell phone in her purse. Clare began to weave her way toward the stairs.

Billy stopped her. "You don't have a glass in your hand, and I'm about to make a toast."

Clare knew how to make a marriage work. You take every opportunity. She said, "Toast? If you get out of my way, in ten minutes, I'll be serving shrimp as big as your mustache."

Billy said, "Perfect. More, more, more," and he let her pass.

Clare and Jeremy disappeared up the stairs.

Billy raised his glass and said, "This is the day we show the rest of the world who we are. We eat a reckless feast. It's in our blood and bones, one heedless day of eating up the better part of the harvest just as the ground hardens and the sun heads south, as if our forefathers knew that, come December, they'd be mincemeat for the gods, so they bowed their heads to the bitter wind and said, 'Fuck you,' and not even a giblet was set aside as a symbol of gratitude or humility—No! The giblets go into the gravy, and nothing is burned and sent heavenward, and to this day, nobody thinks to drop so much as a single squash or pumpkin seed into a pot of dirt as a down payment on next year—No! Even the seeds are washed and roasted and salted and served on the side. I love this day, and I love my brother, Sam, and I would love to see everyone stand up and say, I love America!"

And everyone stood up and shouted, I love America. And then everyone wanted to know if anyone else had ever met Sam's brother, and didn't he live in Mexico, and were there really shrimp? Billy and Sam held court around the coffee table, and Scot joined me in the kitchen, where he was finally allowed to tie on the knee-length white chef's apron Mildred had presented to him that morning while we she served us muffins, "the last digestible meal I'll have today," she said.

Mildred and the Georges always spent Thanksgiving in Gloucester, with the many North Shore Monterossos, who served "birds and animals they killed with their friends, and the only side dish is a tub of margarine." Mildred shooed Scot upstairs to try on his apron because she wanted to tell me that Andrea Burlington was holding up the renovations on Louisa Bamford's house. "She's got a lawyer," Mildred said, "and she found herself a doctor at Harvard to write a letter to Louisa's family explaining that the mask doesn't protect Andrea from house paint, wood stains, polyurethane—or a good punch in the nose, I'll bet. I had Louisa on the telephone just this morning. She's beside herself. Andrea is angling to be sent to a hotel for a few months. Or some other appropriate compensation. Appropriate?" Mildred made a face that warranted a mask. She forced another muffin on me. "I hate to say so, Eddie, but I had a bad feeling as soon as Louisa told me she was going South. Now we have to face up to it. We have to do something. For our own good."

I wasn't sure what the terms of the battle were, but I knew where the line was being drawn—right down the middle of Finn Street. Mildred was safely ensconced between Joan and Greg at the corner and Sam and me at the dead end. But across the street, we faced Louisa's empty house, the evil Burlingtons, and the unaligned Lost Lovelies, and Mildred figured the Lovelies were Harvard-affiliated and thus in league with Andrea and her doctor. Like a lot of Cambridge residents, Mildred assumed that anybody who wouldn't talk to her worked at Harvard. I said, "What are you proposing?"

"I'm just saying you've got a house that'll need a new coat of paint soon, and so do I. And if Georgie Junior is right, the Koesters are about two rainstorms away from a new roof, and just think what it will cost them to find some *appropriate* insulation."

Mildred was right. We were all being held hostage by the lady in the mask. Andrea might become allergic to our barbecue grill or the stuff Sam sprayed in our shady yard to make grass grow between the moss.

She let me consider the awful possibilities, and then she said, "Gives you a rash just to think about it, huh, Eddie?"

I nodded.

Mildred said, "You talk to Sam and Greg. I'll be around on the weekend, God willing."

Along with the apron, Scot and I left Mildred's with two bags of mini marshmallows, "For your yams," she told Scot, who always followed Mildred's instructions. I explained to him that most of our biggest yam fans were vegetarians, but on one of her brief and unhelpful trips into the kitchen to get Billy more wine or cocktail sauce, Nula assured Scot that vegetarians could eat marshmallows, so we compromised and blanketed one of the two vats of yams with "Mildred's secret ingredient."

The kitchen staff had many visitors. Everyone had arrived with a bowl of something that had to be stirred or drained or dressed, and I put Scot in charge of finding out who brought what, and he would drag the owner into our realm for presentation and approval before he carried the donation into the dining room and set it on the table and selected a serving spoon. There were at least four contributors whom I'd never met, and three of them had arrived with rice salads, which wouldn't win them a return ticket. The other one, Mia, came with white netting on her hat, a vintage yellow party dress, ankle socks, and homemade applesauce with horseradish, so Scot and I both admired her, and we were thrilled when she offered to stick around and make the gravy, "unless I'm just a distraction," she said, in a voice that had been cob-smoked in Virginia.

Scot stammeringly offered Mia his apron, but she declined.

"A girl likes to have a few bits on her dress, here and there," she said, "to let everyone know she's not afraid to get dirty when it's time." She waved a spatula at the turkey. "Now all I need is some flour, some very hot water, and a vodka rocks."

Scot delivered the canister, turned on the burner beneath the kettle, and said, "May I ask for your drink order one more time?"

Mia bent her knees, snorted, and working like a weightlifter, she hauled the turkey out of the pan and onto a platter. "Vodka rocks," she said, examining the juices and jetsam she had to work with, "and tell Billy it's for me, so make it a very generous double."

Scot turned away, but he pivoted back and said, "I forgot your name in all the excitement."

"Mia," she said.

Scot looked at me and said. "I'm gonna need the key later, or should I ask Sam?"

That box? Today?

I said, "The key for the toolbox?" It was no surprise that Mia had inspired Scot's decorative impulses, and Sam had stuck to the don't-ask policy, so I said, "It's on Sam's bureau. Do you need it before dinner?"

Scot looked at the clock. He said, "Carla might come over later. I'll need it then."

I nodded.

He said, "That's a yes?"

I said, "It's your box, Scot."

He nodded. To Mia, he said, "Vodka rocks, coming up," and he sprinted away.

Mia and I were busy and silent for several minutes. Our initial enthusiasm was haunting us. Knowing nothing about each had served us so far. Whoever spoke first took the risk of spoiling the fun.

"You're Ed," Mia said, as if she were assigning me a part in a play. "You're with Sam."

I nodded. "You're with Billy?"

"I was late, so I missed his speech. I was late, in order to miss his speech. I heard it several times on the plane." She poured off the grease from the pan and heated up the rest of the drippings on the stove. "How long has Sam had the beard?"

I said, "Since Scot came. September."

"Oh, it's that sort of a beard," she said. "A landmark. How old is Scot?"

"Eleven," I said. I was decanting the stuffing. We were back to back.

"Well, Ed, I guess everybody wants what you've got—a beard and a boy. Anything else I should know about you?"

I said, "My wineglass is empty."

"Not for long," she said, and she pulled the cork out of a half-empty bottle beside the stove. She leaned my way and poured. "Where's our waiter, anyway? I have to leave soon, and I hate to travel with my tank on empty. My father and his accountant are taking me to dinner at the Copley Plaza—is it a hotel?"

I said, "A beautiful old Boston hotel."

Mia nodded, "Daddy thinks home cooking is vulgar. He had three wives, and he left each one as soon as she slid a kid out of the oven. Finally, he married his bookkeeper. She cooks his books, and he buys her dinner at hotels in Boston and Miami. Or has Billy already bored you with the details?"

I said, "I don't think Billy mentioned that you had a father. Or your name."

She paused to tuck that piece of information under her hat. "Now, pass me that flour." Her juices and scraps were sizzling. "And give us back some of that grease. Pour a quarter of a cup right into the pan." I obliged her. "And then you shake in as much salt and pepper as you and Sam like in your gravy. Go ahead—before I'm done adding water and it's too late to make right on our mistakes." I added plenty. "I'm spending the night with my father. Billy is not. In case you don't know even that much." She waited, smiled, shook a lot more pepper into the pan, and said, "A man in my bed is an automatic deduction from my allowance, and the accountant is always eager to save Daddy some money."

I tried and failed to guess her age. She might have been thirty or fifty. She was such a good actress that it didn't matter, and that's why it interested me. The truth or meaning of everything Mia said was subordinated to the way she said it. I stuck the stuffing into the oven to stay warm.

Mia said, "Can I let the gravy happen slow now, or are we rushing to get this meal into people's mouths?"

I said, "Fifteen minutes or so, and then I'll carve the bird."

Mia said, "You work at a magazine. Art, right? European?"

"Monumental," I said, which was as good an explanation as the subscribers got.

Mia said, "Listen, Ed. I need longer answers, or I need a drink. I'm drying up."

I passed her my wine, and she liked it.

"Got another one for yourself over there?"

I found a glass and topped us both off.

She said, "Often, a man in your position will ask about my place of birth or how I first bumped into Billy."

I doubted even Mia had ever run into a man in my position. Quoting my favorite philosopher, I said, "Billy's not *my* brother."

She licked some gravy off her tasting finger. "Best just to leave the business part of this trip to the brothers, then."

Mia looked like a lot of things—a wedding cake, an ad for the past, or a page out of *Figura*—but she didn't look like a liar, so I said, "What does Billy want?"

She said, "To see if he can help clean up the mess he made here, maybe. Or to check under Sam's beard and see if he still has a brother? And if you were Billy, wouldn't you want to show me off?"

I said, "If I were Billy, I'd have come back for Scot."

Mia said, "Would you be doing that to improve Scot's life or to improve Billy's character? And before you answer, you'll want to know that if you were Billy, you'd be standing in the doorway behind yourself right now."

Billy waved.

"What a mess," Mia said, and then she shot the rest of her wine and rinsed her hands. She dried them on her dress. "It's all gravy. Now I'm late for dinner, which is the sort of lapse in manners that can cost me a fortune." She kissed me and whispered, "Say something nice about his little beard," and she kissed Billy and said, "Call me after dinner, and let me know where I can find you tomorrow," and then she was gone.

Billy said, "We haven't said hello yet."

I said, "Hello, Billy." I felt like Scot, who was probably upstairs nursing a vodka rocks.

"I'm glad you met Mia." Billy seemed to think he wanted to shake my hand or embrace me, but somewhere midstep he balked and backed into the counter. "I asked Sam about staying the night."

Up close, I could see he was wearing one of his tailor-made white shirts, but the starch had long since gone out of it, and Billy himself looked soft and slouchy, as if his whole body had been draped over a hanger that was too small. I said, "I have to carve the turkey," but I didn't move.

Billy said, "Just a night or two, Ed. There are some things I have to discuss with Sam."

I said, "Scot lives here, Billy. This is his home."

Billy didn't take this as a rebuke, as it was intended. "Who do you think made sure Scot got here? I did what I could do for him. Found him a home. He'd have hated living with me. Christ, I hate living with me. I knew he'd be safe here. It was what I could do for him, so I did it. And I was right. Wasn't I?"

Yes?

If you put a baby in a Dumpster, you get arrested. If you put a baby in a basket and ship him off to the home of the Pharaoh, you get a place in history. Billy certainly deserved something for depositing Scot on Finn Street, but what?

Billy said, "Do you want me to get Scot's okay?"

I didn't explain that Scot had lost his admitting privileges after the flophouse incident. I said, "I want you to tell me what you want, Billy."

"I want to stop lying to myself. And I don't trust myself with the truth anymore. So I just want to come clean to Sam. On all fronts."

It was the first thing I'd ever heard Billy say that had the force of truth. And because it was Thanksgiving Day, and there were thirty people in the house, and I hadn't carved the turkey yet, and Nula was standing behind him in the doorway to the kitchen with an unlit cigarette in her hand, and she was not backing off, Billy chose this moment to say, "I fucked up. I've got a lot of debts, and I don't know which ones to pay back and which ones to ignore. I'm going back to D.C. to sit behind a computer screen at the State Department because I finally figured out that I'm not Che Guevara. I didn't even bump into him at the embassy cocktail parties. It's amazing, because all I really ever had going for me was Latin America, but in all the time I've spent there, it has never once lived up to my expectations. Except for the incredibly cheap maid service. I expected the whole continent to do my wash, make my breakfast, and be transformed by my ideas about populist democracies. And pick up the tab for my dinners at French restaurants. I've got a lot of certificates from the assistant secretaries of something in Santiago and Quito. A portfolio without an ambassador."

Nula tucked the cigarette over her ear and slipped away. Billy shrugged. "So far, I've managed to get myself a truly stupid little job back in D.C., and I'm taking it. I'm starting again, starting over. What do I want? I don't want to do it all alone."

One of the rice salad strangers joined us. She said she needed balsamic vinegar, though she really needed to learn to make potato salad.

A tall boy wearing a baseball cap and white socks on his hands came in looking for a glass of water.

I said, "I'm Ed."

"I'm Anton," the kid said. He had a goofy smile that made you feel like you were the one with the socks on your hands. "Scot invited me over."

I said, "Does Scot know you're here?"

Anton laughed. "Scot and me are playing in his room, and he said it's after four o'clock, and I was supposed to take my Ritalin or else I'll get out of hand. Sam already invited me for turkey. You can call my grandmother. Sam did." He removed his sock to take his pill, which he pulled from a plastic bag in his pocket. He said, "Later," and he split.

Billy said, "Is it always like this here?"

Robert and Danny arrived at the head of a long line of tidy guests carrying wineglasses and forks and empty platters, all of which we needed for the next round. Nula zipped in and rolled up the blue sleeves of her extra-large silk shirt, and from her helm at the sink she ordered everyone around until the kitchen was shipshape again. Billy headed for the back porch, and I gave him a wide berth, but he sidled up beside me as he passed and said, "We can talk later. I know I owe you." He headed toward the back door, but he changed directions again and walked back into the crowded living room.

I found a carving knife, but Nula said my name sharply and shook her head. She pulled Danny in beside her as a replacement, took the knife out of my hand, and gave it to Robert, and said, "Shrinks rarely get a chance to prove they went to medical school."

Robert said, "The turkey?"

Nula said, "The turkey first. That'll give me time to figure out which head goes on which platter. If Sam is looking for Ed, tell him we'll be back in two or three cigarettes." She pushed out the back door. "Fuck that Billy and the hat girl, too," she said, and she led me around the house and across the street. "I've always wanted to sit on that nice porch. It's built for a smoker. Pillars to lean on."

We sat on the sloping deck boards of Louisa Bamford's empty house and stared at the mess we'd left behind. Nula smoked. I leaned. It was a perfect November afternoon—no sun, no clouds, no wind, no leaves on the trees, and no snow on the ground. No weather to speak of.

Nula said, "Maybe I shouldn't have taken your knife away."

"No, that was good," I said. "Before I murder anybody, I like to know exactly why I'm doing it."

"One reason," Nula said, "is neither one of us can stand to listen to me complain about another man I didn't fuck. I can't believe he showed up with a pair of ankle socks. If I had the good sense to leave right now, the past fifteen years would be nothing more than one of my blind dates." She had to light another cigarette.

Since her second divorce, Nula had a perfect record of abandoning blind dates after the appetizer. She had specific cue lines. If he asked about her favorite anything—color, music, author, movie—she put ten bucks on the table and took a taxi home. Her other prompts included Club Med stories, season tickets to anything ("a prepaid excuse not to call you most weekends"), the phrase "chat room," and questions about the origin of her name.

She had achieved ignition. "Another reason to kill Billy is because he doesn't have a dump permit. He's relentless. You got the kid, and now you get the shambles of his career, and I'm betting you're about to get a few unpaid bills."

I never made any money betting against Nula.

"And there's another thing," Nula said. "Or are we not going to document your losses on this fine day?"

We were quiet and thoughtful for a few minutes. Nula smoked for both of us.

I said, "It's the end of my terrible fantasy."

Nula said, "I know. It's like Marco refusing to fire us. We're going to be editing articles about cupolas and bridges till we die. Our problem is that our enemies are incompetent. Even Sylvia ends up inviting us to Padua."

I nodded. "Until today, there was always the chance that Billy—"

Nula said, "I know. I know." She didn't want me to have to say it. "A chance—heaven forfend—that Billy would bust down the door and announce that he was taking the kid away."

I said, "A slim chance, I admit, but I found I could beef it up into a pretty impressive battle scene. And I got to be very good at fighting for Scot, defending my honor and Sam's, and—"

"Did you ever lose?" Nula flicked her filter into the street.

"Did I ever lose Scot?" I nodded. "Hard as I fought, I did."

Nula needed one more half-cigarette.

I said, "A while ago, you threatened to tell me something terrible about your growing up. Something so bad it would make me feel good."

Nula nodded. "I was bluffing. Sorry. You win again."

twenty-two

A good long day works on you just like wine, particularly if you drink wine all day long. By the time we ate, it was so late and Sam was so happy, that he took the tofu off the table and replaced it with Robert and Danny's traditional gift to us all—two quarts of mayonnaise and several packages of sliced white bread. Many people skipped the whole hot-meal ordeal and treated themselves to complicated sandwiches instead. Almost no one failed to scoop out a side of enhanced yams.

I wanted to congratulate Scot, but he wasn't with us. I saw Anton. He was standing on the stairs, hiding his face in his hands. When I walked up and past him, he looked away and slowly descended, so I figured I would find Scot in his bedroom with his hair in curlers and cotton balls between his painted toes. But to my surprise, Scot had not enhanced his appearance. He was leaning against a wall, just thinking, tying a few extra knots in the knotted strings on either side of his apron. There was no space for either of us to sit. He had dumped the contents of the toolbox onto his bed, and his empty wooden hygiene case, which normally housed the collection of personal-sized grooming products that Nula had stolen for him from hotels and the bathrooms of her well-traveled friends, was occupying the only chair. He said, "I might have to get rid of some old stuff and store it in the basement. Like the pajamas."

I nodded my approval.

He also wanted to know if I had ever worn aprons "in the olden days, when you used to be a painter."

I was a painter once, or twice, and I kept some old easels and empty wooden frames in the cellar, where Scot had recently spent his probationary period poking his nose into the past. I told him I used to wear big old shirts when I painted.

"Like Nula?" Scot asked.

"Not as nice," I said, but he had the scale right.

"Not so silky?"

I nodded.

Scot said, "Cotton smocks?"

It was a phrase he had heard—maybe from Julie, maybe in a filmstrip about Rembrandt—and he was testing it to see if it was one of the things you can say or one of the things you can't. "Sort of," I said. "Yes. You could call them that." I probably had called them that when I called myself a painter.

Scot nodded. Cotton smocks. Acceptable. So noted. He surveyed his bed, then the crowded floor of his closet, and then my face. "Are you looking for something, Ed?"

I said, "I was looking for you, Scot."

"Okay," he said. That was good enough for him.

"It's time to eat," I said. "Wait'll you see. Everyone loves Mildred's yams."

"It's the mini marshmallows," he said.

"You were right," I said. "Next year, we'll use both bags."

"Thanks for telling me," he said. Then he smiled. "Apology accepted."

"Thanks," I said.

Before we left his room, Scot tucked the knotted strings of his apron into his pants, and I looked for clues among the scattered makeup and shampoos, a hint about the future, a glimpse of what Scot would make of himself. But on Thanksgiving Day, all that came of the mess on the bed was an eyebrow-pencil mustache for Anton, who giggled and blushed every single time somebody bothered to tell him that he needed a shave.

The only deep disappointment of the day was the failed fire, and Danny had convinced almost everyone that Barbara was to blame. "Robert and I couldn't get a twig in edgewise," he complained while the rest of us were elbowing our way toward the gravy. "And if you don't believe me, Donna will testify on my behalf."

Donna refused to take the stand.

Barbara left the dining room. She was gnawing on a turkey wing. She said, "This case is not closed," and left to her own devices, she built a bonfire. When we were all packed into the living room with our plates and forks and we were trying to find smooth, steady surfaces for cups of tea and glasses of wine, Barbara struck a single wooden match, and a big blast of flame boomed up the chimney, and for a moment there we all expected the house to rise like a rocket from its foundation.

Danny accused her of soaking her kindling in gasoline, and she had been seen outside a few minutes earlier, leaning against a car with a section of the newspaper, but she claimed she'd been reading her horoscope.

Barbara took a victory lap or two around the dining room table and collected her spoils, and everything that happened and didn't happen after that was laced with tryptophan and wood smoke and the odor of inevitability. Billy was staying for the night, maybe two, and Liz Morita called in Joey's regrets to Scot's invitation to join us for dessert, and almost as soon as Nula and Sam went out to fix Nula's car, a police cruiser arrived with its lights flashing. Carla's father, Desmond, was a cop. They stayed long enough for Scot to teach Carla how to cover up her zits "without causing any hypo-allergies," long enough for Danny to fulfill his fantasy of serving pie and whipped cream to a man with a gun, long enough to see several guests stagger to their feet and shuffle home without their lidded bowls, but not quite long enough to watch Nula race around with a sponge and a broom and a postcard and finally dump the rice salad and the unsmoked joints into the disposal and say, "Do me one favor. After I climb in, hit the switch."

twenty-three

I left Billy and Sam on the sofas. Scot was asleep. His boxes were locked. I had two tasks to dispose of: Billy's bed and Billy's forged letters, which I had never read.

There was a light on in the spare room. When I pushed open the door, I could see that Scot had been there before me. He had dragged the futon to the middle of the room and unfolded it. It was rather gaily outfitted with an ancient set of yellow-striped sheets, Scot's red-and-white checked bedspread, and two folded rust wool blankets still sealed in the dry cleaner's plastic but beautified by a few well-placed rainbow stickers. There were five after-dinner mints on the pillow. Two baby blue bath towels hung from the StairMaster, as did a soap on a rope. Other grooming necessities, including a vanilla votive candle, were lined up on the small bureau, with a note: "No charge for using up the supplies."

Such accommodations.

Five mints and a fluffed-up pillow; that's what you get for abandoning Scot.

I closed the door halfway.

I read the letters, which Sam kept in a plastic sleeve in his sock drawer. In both of them, he was referred to as "Samuel," which you might assume was his legal name, but not if you were his brother you wouldn't. Julie had written the letters. In the first, Julie is just Julie, and she asks Samuel and Edward to be her son's guardians in the event of her death; it was written one year before Julie and Billy actually made the request. The second letter was dated one week later. In it, Julie is pretending to be Samuel, who enthusiastically and humbly and cordially—and in many other un-Samly terms—accepts the assignment.

Why had Julie insisted that we get Scot? Why had Billy participated in the hoax? They could have just asked. A year later, they did ask. It was complicated and conspiratorial and pointless. Almost Italian.

I closed my eyes, which was easier than trying to close the door on the past.

twenty-four

I had an hour of my own in the kitchen, which was big with the white morning sunshine and no food on the counters and everyone who was not there. The floor was cold, and a slowly brewing second pot of coffee was the only incense in the air. I had not read the paper, but above the Gothic lettering of the masthead I had made several little sketches of a leafless maple tree. Once a year, for almost twenty years, I had driven west to photograph, and sketch, and sometimes paint a single tree in Lenox, in the Berkshires, and I had about a month left to decide if I would finally give it up, loosen the last knot in that apron string.

When I went up to use the bathroom, I peeked into Scot's room, and his bed was empty, so I sat down on the shirt and pants on his chair and waited. And waited. Whatever part of himself he was waxing or curling or deodorizing, it was awfully quiet. Maybe he was as nervous about waking Billy as I was.

145

I stood outside the bathroom. Nothing. I wasn't sure I wanted to see what he was up to, but there was no spill of light beneath the door, and that made me suspicious. Scot usually operated with all the electrical systems on high—lights, fan, blow-dryer, Sam's vibrating toothbrush, and sometimes a flashlight, too, for those hard-to-see places.

I knocked twice, pushed open the door, and his tooth-brush was on the rim of the bathtub, and there were three or four inches of blue toothpaste on the floor beside the sink, and the tube was standing in the plastic cup that hung beside the mirror. Scot had been there in the last hour, but he was not there now. It was not absolutely impossible to believe that he had accidentally flushed himself down the toilet, but I thought I ought to check his closet before I called a plumber. Then I heard Billy's snoring. It was even louder when I opened up the medicine cabinet and leaned in over the sink.

In the hall, I opened Billy's door, just a little. Scot was lying on the futon, nestled under Billy's arm. He was sleeping, or else he was a very good faker.

He had never asked to sleep in our bed.

He had never been invited.

It was almost half an hour before Scot joined me in the kitchen. He was wearing his nightshirt, and his breath was minty fresh. As I poured him a bowl of cereal, he said, "Billy's still asleep. He's curled up like a cat." We flipped through pages of the paper, and when the telephone rang Scot picked it up and said, "Oh, hi." He listened for a while, and then he said, "Ed says hello, too," though I hadn't, and he covered the receiver and whispered, "It's Mia. She sounds lonely." When he rejoined me at the table, he said, "She'll call back at noon. She didn't want to leave a number."

Above his head, there was a nail in the wall. Usually, Julie was hanging behind him.

Scot said, "Do cats have nine lives, or is that just exaggeration?"

We were both done with the newspaper, and I hid my sketches at the bottom of the pile. I said, "I think cats are good at escaping from danger. When they fall out of a window, or you think they're under the tires of a car—"

Scot raised his hand and said, "I get it. I get it, already." He didn't need the gory details. He cleared and wiped the table, but he left me my coffee cup, which he kindly refilled. Then he pulled the silverware tray out of the dishwasher and fitted the knives and forks and serving spoons into their drawers. "What do you wanna do today, Ed?"

We both knew Billy and Sam would want to talk, and it was a cold day, so I suggested ice skating. Scot was intrigued, but as soon as I mentioned renting skates, he had to pee. When he returned, he stood beside the dishwasher and passed me the holiday plates and cups, and I stacked them in the high and hard-to-reach cabinets. He said he'd been to a bowling party once and spent the afternoon in a smelly, slippery pair of shoes that did not match. "The old guy at the counter made me take one with racing stripes on the side and one with no stripes, and it threw off my balance. A couple of kids started calling me Crazy Horse every time I tried to roll the ball. If you don't mind, can we just stop at the bank and I'll buy my own skates?"

I told him we'd figure it out after we showered and chose a museum.

Scot said, "So I should bring my notebook?"

"And a pencil," I said. "And if you're quick up there, we'll have time to get a croissant at the Heyday on our way."

Scot said, "I'll be quick as a cat."

I nodded. Almost every week I dragged him to a different museum or gallery, and we'd worked out a system for staying longer than five minutes and less than an entire morning or afternoon. Another compromise. Scot had to find five items that somehow matched something we'd seen in another museum. Sprinkler systems, food in the coffee-shop display case, and other patrons did not count. Our field trips gave Sam a chance to schedule evening or weekend clients, and they gave me a chance to shop for Scot-equivalents among the other oddly dressed, well-behaved children whose parents or guardians or baby-sitters wanted them to know that before Picasso started to appear on posters in the mall as a model for chinos, he'd squandered his time and his figure in a cotton smock.

It was after nine o'clock, and I wanted to get on with the day and get out of the house. Billy made me nervous, and I knew that both Scot and I had been spared the full force of him so far. On Thanksgiving, his charms and wiles had been depleted by the plane ride, intensive preparations for his big speech, and the crowd. I dreaded a private confrontation, and Billy seemed to be fortifying himself with a threateningly good long sleep.

I knew that Billy was unreliable, and I knew that Sam's affection for Billy was reliable, and I knew that the combination threw off my balance, but when I got upstairs, Scot was just getting into the shower, Sam was meditating on the floor by our bed, Julie was glaring at me from Scot's bureau, and Billy was banging around in his bedroom, so I hurried back down the stairs to call Nula, but Scot had made the telephone disappear again. Sometimes he brought it to school in his lunch bag, and sometimes he slipped it into the recycling bin. I found it on the dryer in the basement and called Nula from below ground level, but she didn't interrupt her other conversation to talk to me, so I hung up, let it ring twice, hung up again and let it ring three times, and she said, "I've got Eleanor Covena on the other line, and she did it. Or they did it. She's so mad, I can't tell yet if she quit or resigned or got fired. First of the year. First of the year. That's all I know. I'm sure it won't make a damn bit of difference, but somehow I see some new chairs in our future, and if we really put the squeeze on, we'll get heat."

I said, "We'll also probably get Sylvia."

"No Italian is stupid enough to move to America, Ed."

I said, "Sylvia is English."

Nula said, "You obviously weren't paying attention to her shoes. Call me later."

I was losing a colleague, but I was more interested in counting my gains, which included fifteen or twenty ant traps Scot had stuck on the ledges and windowsills he'd cleaned. They formed a trail that ended near the furnace, where he had nailed up an old sheet diagonally across a corner of the wooden shelves. He'd safety-pinned a sign to the curtain: "Please do not enter. Not finished yet."

Behind that drape lurked an alternative environment. What sort of a home had Scot made for himself? For a moment, I hoped the project had been inspired by the dioramas we'd both admired at Harvard's museum of natural history. But it smelled piney, and the shelving—scrap lumber studs and planks—suggested the unfinished interior of a dollhouse. It was depressing to think what that would mean for Christmas.

I didn't open the curtain. He wasn't finished yet.

I ran into Billy in the kitchen. He was brushing his teeth above the breakfast bowls and cups Scot had stacked in the sink. He was wearing boxer shorts and his wrinkled white shirt. After he spit, he said, "I can't believe you guys only have one bathroom. How'd you sleep?"

"There's coffee," I said.

"What I really want is bacon and eggs," he said. "That's what I missed most about the States."

"There's orange and grapefruit juice in the refrigerator," I said.

"Is it fresh?" Billy sat down, presumably to make it easier for me to serve him.

"There's also ten pounds of old tofu in the oven," I said.

Billy said, "You and Scot already eat?"

I said, "Mia's calling back at noon. Scot and I are going out for the day. Do you need the bathroom before I shower?"

Billy nodded.

I said, "I'll get Scot out now," and I left.

Upstairs, Scot was brushing his teeth again. He was wearing a towel turban, which meant he still hadn't combed his hair, so I gave him " one more minute." He tied on a matching towel sarong and rushed back to his bedroom to complete the morning ministrations.

Billy ducked into the bathroom with a towel. He was going to take a shower, which meant either Sam or I would be treated to a cold-water rinse, and I was not feeling generous.

Before I closed myself into the bedroom with Sam, Scot yelled, "Which jacket should I wear? The pullover poncho with the zipper pockets?"

"With a sweater and a turtleneck," I said, "and the jeans with the flannel lining."

Scot said, "Layered look. Okay. White socks?"

"And bring an extra pair of the heavy ones," I said. "And a hat and mittens."

Scot said, "Okay. Remind me about the hat and mittens before we leave, okay?"

"Okay," I said.

"Okay," he said.

Almost every day.

Sam was sitting on the bed, staring at the stand of pine trees that hemmed us in at the dead end of Finn Street. His white shirt was stuck to several wet splotches on his back, and water was dripping from his hair to his collar. "I jumped into the shower while Scot was flossing," he said.

I could hear Billy enjoying the last of the hot water. I said, "We're going to a gallery and then ice skating, God help me."

Sam said, "What inspired that?"

I said, "Something in the air today."

Sam turned quickly, as if I'd said something odd or profound. "There's a lot in the air today," he said. "You finally read those letters?"

"I did," I said.

Sam said, "Billy told me more of the story last night."

I didn't need to know the gory details. What lay behind those letters was between Sam and Billy. He was not my brother.

Sam said, "I need to talk to you, Ed."

"Okay," I said, but Sam didn't sound okay.

He said, "Alone," as if we weren't. "Last night, when Liz Morita called, she asked if we'd let Scot sleep over there tonight. I think I'll call her and say yes. Don't you think Scot would like that?"

The Moritas had all of the old *Star Trek* episodes on tape. Who wouldn't like that?

Sam said, "Billy wants an adjustment and then, depending on the timing, I thought maybe we could have dinner with him and Mia tonight."

"Here?"

Sam said, "Chinese?"

I nodded. Anything for Peking duck.

Sam said, "I'll go talk to him about going to Joey's now. Okay?" He didn't move.

"Do you want to say something else?"

Sam said, "To you? Now?"

Everything either of us said sounded stilted, as if we weren't supposed to talk until we had our talk.

I said, "I should shower now, right? Are you okay?"

Sam said, "No, so try to be home by two or so."

We heard Billy in the hall.

Sam said, "By two, then?"

I said, "At the latest."

"That helps," he said, and he grabbed me hard and kissed my hair. "It looks really cold out there today. Wear a hat."

It was cold. But after Scot and I found a parking meter, I let the engine idle, and we sat in the warm car in our sweaters and turtlenecks eating our croissants, so neither of us wanted to bother with our coats, and we ran to the door of the new storefront gallery in North Cambridge I'd picked out for us.

Scot said, "It's locked."

The place was dark. I tried the handle.

Scot said, "I know how to open a door, Ed."

I said, "What should we do?"

Scot said, "Can we discuss it in the car, please?"

With hot air blowing on our faces and feet, I think we both wanted to go home and sit on the sofas in front of the fire and eat turkey sandwiches. But I wanted Scot to know how it felt to move effortlessly across ice, so I told him we'd only do it if he could rent figure skates, and the man behind the counter produced a matching pair, and for a few memorable minutes, I skated backward and pulled him by the arms around the rink.

In the middle of our fifth loop, he said, "It might be fun to stop for a while, too." The rink was not too crowded, and most people were circling slowly, leaving plenty of space for shaky and tired skaters to hang on the boards. A few young girls were spinning and jumping in the middle, and a few others occasionally inched away from the pack and attempted something fancy, and usually they crash-landed, brushed off their jeans, and then raced to catch up to their friends. An old man in a baseball cap skated smoothly with his hands behind his back. And one kid in racing skates and a skullcap whizzed around very near the boards with his extra-long, extra-whiny blades, barking "Aside! Aside!"

Scot was able to stand up with only one hand on the boards, and he'd figured out how to use his serrated tips as brakes. His poncho was causing him some problems, though. When we were moving, I'd thought it was puffed up with wind, but now I could see he had stuffed something into every one of the zippered pockets, even on the arms and in the back.

He said, "Go skate, Ed. I'm having fun," and then he fell.

I helped him up. He was packing at least twenty extra pounds.

The speed skater yelled, "Off the ice!" and sprayed us with some shavings.

Scot yelled, "Quit it!" He fell again, and this time he almost did the splits. "This is trickier than I thought," he said. He reached for my hand. "But it's still fun."

The bird of prey swooped by again. "Off the ice!"

As he fell, Scot yelled, "Quit it!"

I heard something crack.

Scot look more curious than hurt. He said, "I wonder what that was?"

The speedster hopped over the boards and joined two friends in the bleachers, so we had a chance to have an uninterrupted, upright conversation. I said, "Do you want to sit down for a while?"

Scot was more interested in the jumping, twirling girls at center ice. He dared to raise his right foot, and he stuck it out behind himself, but when his one wavering blade started to move, he dropped the act and grabbed my arms. That was a leap he would never make. "It must be fun," he said. He was smiling and sad.

I said, "How about we empty a few of your pockets? It might make it easier to balance."

Scot raised his free arm, and we both watched the bulges shift. "I'm fine," he said.

"What do you have in there?"

Scot said, "In where?"

I said, "In your jacket."

"Oh, that," he said. "Chapstick."

I didn't say anything.

He shrugged. "Probably one package of travel tissues."

I nodded.

"Just some Band-Aids and after-dinner mints. Want one?"

"No thanks," I said.

"I didn't know if it was outdoors, so sunglasses."

I nodded.

He closed his eyes before he said, "A pack of cards. Matches. Two extra pair of socks." He opened his eyes. The socks were not his fault, not both pairs.

I looked at his ankles, which were almost touching the ice.

The speed skater was back in action.

Scot said, "A kitchen spoon. A chocolate pudding snack, which might be leaking, I think. Did I say Band-Aids?"

After the inventory, Scot said he'd skate until he felt like playing solitaire. He was only fifteen feet from an exit to the bleachers, and for a few minutes he did stand, and he even took several steps on his serrated tips, moving on the ice, if not quite skating, until the racer started to circle and scare him again, and then Scot sat down and began to hand-paddle himself to safety.

I skated to his rescue.

Scot said, "I'm having fun, Ed. Go on."

I said, "You stay on the ice. I'll talk to that kid."

"Don't," he said. He crawled into the bleachers. "He just wants to prove he's better at skating."

I said, "He's not any better than anybody else."

Scot took off his hat, felt his staticky hair, and stuck the hat back on. "I ran out of conditioner," he said. "This isn't my sport, Ed. But it was a good try."

The terrorist flew by. I said, "I'd like to trip that guy."

"Quit it, Ed. He's not worth it." Scot was fishing something out of his poncho, and by the time we were in the car, we'd eaten all the chocolate mints, the pudding, and we'd both applied a thick coat of raspberry Chapstick.

The house was dark, and as we peeled off a few layers in the living room, Scot said, "Do you think Mrs. Burlington's mask really works?"

"She seems to think so," I said.

Scot was staring at the Burlington house and blinking one eye at a time, to make it move from side to side. He said, "I don't think she has any friends. You never see them."

Andrea Burlington. Our Miss Schoop. A fanatic. As my father might have said, I said, "Some people don't want to make friends."

Scot squinted, making Andrea's house almost disappear. He said, "Aren't you glad now you didn't trip that speed racer?"

"Yes," I said, though I wasn't. I would always want to trip anyone who noticed the weakness I noticed in Scot.

"Me, too," he said, "and I'm sorry we got locked out of the museum." But he wasn't.

Scot volunteered to take a hot bath, and I heated up some yams and gravy, piled bread and turkey onto a platter, set us two places on the coffee table, and built a fire. I found Scot's favorite CD and turned it up loud, so he could hear it while he soaked. The performer was a pretty young girl with bangs and a bad attitude about her bad luck with bad lovers, and she sounded like every singer Scot admired. She sounded like Joni Mitchell's cat. I listened alone to seven cuts of her mewing and yowling, and finally Scot came dancing down the stairs in a pair of blue jeans and a black sweater I had never seen. He said, "Thanks for the mood music, Ed."

We ate a lot of lunch. We watched the fire. I asked him about the sweater.

He said, "This? It's just something Billy let me try on, and we liked the way it fit. It's from somewhere in Peru, or even farther down there. It's soft. From somewhere in Billy's past."

twenty-five

Billy was in Boston with Mia. Sam was in the kitchen making tea. Scot was waiting by the living room windows in his poncho and mittens. He'd packed his nightshirt, a toothbrush, and the rest of the after-dinner mints into his red wool hat, because "Joey's got two bags belonging to me already, and Sam says I can't afford to lose any more." I was sitting on my sofa, sipping cold coffee. It tasted like raspberry yams.

I went upstairs to gargle and brush, and I heard a car horn, and the door slammed shut several times, and by the time I was done, Sam had set his biggest ceramic pot on the living room table with three cups, a notebook, and a pen. He'd also done something to bring the fire back to life.

Sam half-filled two of the cups.

I said, "Are we waiting for someone else?"

Sam turned the other cup upside-down.

He sipped.

I sipped.

That's why people invent rituals—to express the ineffable.

twenty-six

It was more than a moment of silence. The living room was vast, as if the Thanksgiving crowd had pushed all the walls out of the way and raised the ceiling, and it might be weeks before the house fit us again. Even the empty sofas seemed superfluous. And the upside-down cup was a symbol, like a nail in a wall where a picture once hung. Sam stared at the fire, and several times he squinted and almost said something, but the smallest spark or snapping flame would stop him, and he sipped his tea instead, swallowing the thoughts, which were bitter, I could tell, and did not go down easily. This time together, this talk we were not having, seemed mournful and ceremonial and too well planned. Sam had arranged it all—the appointed hour, the tea, and Scot's departure. And just when Sam was ready to speak, a big truck rumbled down the street. We stared out the window where Scot had stood, and for a few minutes more we watched two men carry furniture and boxes out of the Burlington house. Somebody was moving somewhere. I didn't know who was coming or going in their house, but the moving men were an omen, and sometimes you don't have to squint to see the future. It is before you. Like an unused cup.

Sam said, "Changes," and he sat back from the edge of his sofa and tried to smile.

Apparently, the tea ceremony was complete.

I said, "Say it, Sam. What does Billy want?"

Sam said, "Billy and Mia both want what's best for Scot."

I said, "Billy's not Scot's father. Right?"

"No." Sam was speaking slowly, gauging my capacity and my willingness to absorb the truth. He said, "But Scot has a brother." And the significance of that word in Sam's vocabulary, the trueness of that bond, that brotherly way of feeling he was not alone in the world, was so big that Sam said it again. "A brother."

Billy had come back, and Scot had climbed into bed beside him, and now there was a brother. And a gravy-making woman with a hat. By comparison, even I could see that two guardians and a spare room looked provisional.

I said, "A half brother?"

Sam nodded. "Billy and Julie had a child when Scot was six."

I said, "Scot doesn't know?"

Sam said, "Not yet."

Not yet. Not yet. Why not never? I said, "So, Julie had two sons. Billy got one, and we got one. End of story. Julie is dead."

"It's not as simple as it sounds," Sam said.

I said, "Where is this half brother?"

Sam said, "His name is Corey."

I said, "Where is this half brother?"

Sam said, "Stop calling him a half."

I said, "After you pour Scot some tea."

"Mia adopted Corey," Sam said. "She's had him since the day he was born."

"That almost makes her Corey's mother," I said, "but not nearly Scot's. Pour the tea."

Sam said, "Mia is Corey's mother. Corey is Scot's brother. And Billy—"

"Billy is back, right? For how long, Sam? How long this time? Pour the tea."

Sam didn't move. He looked at me meditatively. He said, "It's just tea, Ed. And if you calm down and let me try to—"

I yelled, "Try not calming down for a change, Sam. Try telling your brother he's fucked up enough lives, and time has passed. Time has passed, and it's too late—"

"We're not talking about the past," Sam said. "I'm talking about Scot. And Billy has known him since he was two, and he—"

Still too loudly, I said, "Please, Sam," and I stood up, and just like that, I was sadder, and I said, "Just for now, just turn over his cup. Pour the tea." But something else was rising in me, something innate and rational and inevitable, and I could count the days Scot had been with us, and it was only three months, three pages of a calendar, and the year was running out, and the big Christmas break was coming, and then it would be a new year, and now was the time to prepare him for a new life with a little brother and a man who had known him almost forever and a woman who could adopt him and raise him in a house where everyone had one name.

Sam looked shaken, but his voice was smooth, and his eyes were half-closed when he said, "I'll pour him some tea."

And he did. And it was too late. From now on, it was just tea.

Sam said, "I don't know what to say to you, Ed."

And I wanted to cry, and I didn't want to cry, and it was all out of my confused loyalty to Scot, so I said, "Take a note. Write this down. I never wanted a kid. But you saw that there was room here," and that did it. I was crying, because from now on there would be too much room in the house, and in my heart and there would always be that extra cup in a cabinet that I would have to open every day. "And you said he would grow. You said you would notice him every day. You touched your heart and said it, Sam. You were talking for me, too. I might never be a proper painter, but I'm telling you, when I look at that kid, I'm Giotto. I can see he has a future. And it's golden. And I cannot put it down on paper. I don't have the hands. You do, Sam. You have the hands. Please don't let him go."

Sam was crying, too, or trying not to, and when he looked at me, he waved his hand, because he couldn't speak, but I knew it meant, stop. Please stop.

But stopping was conceding, so I said, "You can tell yourself and everyone we know about brothers and families and how it worked out so well in the end. But today is not the end. Today it's Billy's sweater, and Billy's arm around his back, and don't you see? That's how it was for me. Someone else, and someone else, and with or without his bracelets or a brother, he will always find a way to prove that no one can accommodate him. Somewhere, Scot had a mother and a father. It didn't turn out normal, and neither did he. But there was room for him here, Sam, just between you and me."

I was spent, but I was standing, and the longer Sam was silent, the harder it was to imagine what I should do next.

Sam said, "Will you listen to me now?"

And that moved me. I turned and ran up the stairs, taking them two at a time, and that is when you take your kid and grab his coat and ditch the car at the bus station and go far, far, far away until you run out of old friends and disguises and alibis and you hope you are underground, so far below the recognizable surface of your former life that you are safe, and nothing more can change, and nothing can be lost or taken away.

Or at least you understand how it happens.

I ran myself a bath, in homage to Scot. And I was cold. As I sat soaking in the hot water, I had nothing to say to myself. Maybe that's the meaning of transcendental meditation. I listened to the screeching dollies of the moving men. There was music of the Scot variety seeping across the street from the radio in their idling truck. I opened one of Scot's big plastic jars, and I picked out and sniffed the yellow, green, and purple fruit-scented bubble-bath balls. I loved the kid, but I didn't want to smell like sangria.

Sam walked in with his big ceramic pot and poured the tea, leaves and all, into the tub. He said, "That shit Scot uses will only dry out your skin more." He put the teapot on the hamper and opened the medicine cabinet. He pulled out a pair of scissors and said, "I know Billy pretty well, and I know that Scot will do well to have a brother. It will give Scot another way to know who he isn't."

I didn't want to talk about it. I didn't want to hear about it. But getting out and past Sam was not going to be easy, and if there was a struggle, someone would be hurt.

Sam's hand was a little shaky, but he clipped a few hairs from his beard, and then he said, "I believe every word you said about Scot." Then he put the scissors on the sink and stared at his reflected image. He said, "You see us all so beautifully. And for the record, take a note. You're right." He smiled, and he clipped the bottom of his beard. "And I'm so far and away and deeply in love with you, that sometimes I forget . . ." He bowed his head.

I said, "Sam, you don't have to say it."

Sam nodded. He whispered, "I do have to say it."

I said, "Okay. You forget what?"

Sam said, "I forget what an asshole you can be," and he giggled, and then it was so funny he had to brace himself on the sink and laugh out loud. He turned to me and shook his head, and even though he looked crazy, I could tell he thought I was the crazy one when he said, "Give Scot away? To Billy? I wouldn't let Billy borrow my car. And I would give away my hands before I would give that kid away. Where do you come up with this stuff? Have I ever said anything that would even hint at the possibility that I would be willing to entertain even the hypothetical notion that in the event of a catastrophe of inhuman proportions—"

"Okay! Uncle!" It was evident that I had made a few big illogical leaps and ended up in a tub full of tea, but I didn't think Sam had to rub it in. I was already beginning to smell like a Peking duck. I said, "But the tea. What was all that business with the tea?"

Sam said, "What business?"

I said, "The three cups, and the one you turned over, and the way you solemnly poured—"

"It was tea," Sam said. He pointed at the pot.

I said, "Tea?"

Sam said, "Tea. I brought out a cup for Scot, and then Liz and Joey showed up. And I was trying to get my mind around the whole Billy and Mia saga so I could spare you the six-hour version Billy told me, and then the moving van came back to the Burlington house, and the men started to take away boxes and chairs after they'd been dumping stuff into the house all morning, and then you—"

"I thought you were trying to tell me something," I said.

"I could tell," Sam said. "Whenever you think I'm trying to tell you something, you do most of the talking."

"You should've stopped me," I said. "You should always stop me."

"I tried a few times. And you kept telling me to pour the tea again, and I thought," Sam paused to laugh a little more, and then said, "I thought, but I did that already. I poured the damn tea." His smile faded slowly, and then he had to heave out a big breath to say, "And then you said Scot was golden," and he held his face in his strong hands and wept and said my name between breaths, "Ed," he said, "Ed," and his face was shiny wet, and he was smiling and he said, "I've been waiting for you to say so. To tell me you could see it. We aren't crazy. We'll be fine." Sam shook his head. "Right?"

I nodded.

And then Sam knelt beside the bath and ran his hand right through my hair and said, "The three of us are fine."

twenty-seven

The Giotto painting I so love is one of seven surviving panels of a single altarpiece. Its fellows are scattered, separately held and guarded in museums and private collections around the world. A few were lost. That's the history of treasured things.

Mia saved Julie and Billy's baby, and that made Mia a mother, and it made Corey a survivor, and it may have made a man of Billy.

It was all there in what was not there in the letters Sam kept in his sock drawer.

Scot was six, and Julie was using while she was pregnant, and Billy was using that as his best argument for giving his kid away. He had been with Julie and Scot for four years, and he was ready to go, to leave them behind, and Julie didn't know how else to stop him, so she kept shooting up but stopped taking her birth-control pills, and when she told her old friend Mia that she was going to have Billy's baby, Mia said, "That is going to be one confused kid." She lived in D.C., and she'd only met Billy twice, but Mia was born having seen it all before. Thus her flair for vintage fashion.

"The letters were Julie's idea," Billy said. We were staring at each other from our opposing sofas. Sam and Mia were sharing a seat. We'd ordered enough food for eight people, and I was sure I wouldn't get my fill. I'd eaten seven dumplings and finished the sesame noodles, and Sam had topped off my tea several times and made a stern face to let me know that I should slow down and give everyone else a chance, but when I get hold of chopsticks I play by Halperin Day hockey rules. Lead with the sticks, and just pretend you didn't hear the referee's whistle; somebody will drag you off the pile when you've gone too far.

"The letters were Julie's idea of blackmail," Billy said.

Mia said, "You didn't protect your own kid, Billy. She was trying to protect Scot."

Billy nodded. I was impressed. He'd first reconnected with Mia years ago, when they traveled together to Peru, but their courtship had been tentative and very slow. They'd only been living together for a few months, and already Billy had learned to accept her reproofs. It made me feel there was hope for him, and it also made me want to write down every annoying or stupid thing Billy ever said and then send the list to Mia, just in case she ever ran out of reasons to chastise him. "Julie said if I didn't sign the guardianship letters, she'd start making phone calls to everyone I knew and say I'd made her give away our kid. And it wasn't that simple, but I had given away my son." Billy looked at Sam. Sam nodded. "Well, that's what I did once. For the rest of my life I will have to say, Once, I gave up my son."

Mia said, "once, my father accidentally sent my birthday card to my stepsister in Philadelphia. We'd never even met.

She called me up and said she was sorry, and we became friends. And now Daddy and his bookkeeper are sitting in some red-leather booth trying to make Corey eat lobster thermidor. All that happened once."

Sam said, "Now I want a lobster."

Mia said, "I'll introduce you to Daddy."

Billy had to say what he had to say. "I knew Sam would recognize the letters as a hoax or a fraud, but by the time I was really leaving, the idea of Scot coming here didn't seem so crazy. But it was always just an idea, a contingency. Who knew Julie would die?"

Mia said, "Anyone who didn't have burritos in his ears."

We were all quiet for a minute, and then Mia stood up and reached for the rice, and she shoved the box of dumplings my way. She was wearing teal blue stretch pants with black elastic foot holsters, a white angora sweater, and a red hair band, as if she'd just returned from the 1960 Squaw Valley Winter Olympics. You couldn't help but be grateful.

Billy looked at Sam and said, "Julie was always threatening to kill herself."

Sam said. "That doesn't exactly explain. . . ." and then he shrugged, as if he'd forgotten what he was going to say.

Mia watched Sam for a while, and when he smiled, she put her hand on his back.

The telephone rang, and Billy said, "We really want to bring Corey by tomorrow," as Sam sprang up.

Mia said, "We want to talk about bringing Corey by tomorrow."

Billy said, "That's what I said."

Sam was talking to Scot on the telephone in the kitchen, and he wandered in and said, "So just in case, why don't you say good-bye now. And then if you decide you want to stay for lunch, you won't be sorry." He handed the telephone to Billy and said, "Just in case you don't see him before you leave."

Mia said, "That doesn't explain. . . what, Sam?"

To Scot, Billy said, "Soon. So I guess just good-bye for now, kiddo, huh?"

Sam said, "Nothing."

Mia said, "You're right. It doesn't explain why he left Scot."

Billy said, "Righto," and clicked off. He held the telephone in the air so that someone could more easily take it from him and hang it up.

Mia said, "But Scot was always a separate story—it's a portable, sweetie, but it's not going to fly back to where it belongs, so just lay it on the table."

Billy did. He didn't look angry.

Mia said, "I'd like to say Julie protected Scot. I only know she mostly kept him out of sight."

Sam said, "So Billy said."

I'd always thought of Scot sitting under a table by himself in Baltimore, so it was comforting to imagine Scot and Julie together, secreted inside an imaginary fort, whispering about the enemy.

Sam touched Mia's arm and said, "Billy told you, right? Scot doesn't know about Corey. I think Ed and I need a month or two to talk to Scot about it all before we put the two boys in a room together."

Mia said, "Corey doesn't know Scot lives here with you. I've been vague. And Corey is a vague boy. You need to know that before we start anything. He takes things in well enough, now that we've figured out his hearing. But you know those clothes dryers that seem to work just fine except

they eat a sock or two every time? Corey's brain is like that."
Mia dumped a little bit of rice on everyone's plate, "Before Ed
eats the box," she said.

And at ten in the morning, just half a day later, while Scot
was still with Joey sleeping off his sleep-over, Corey sat next
to Billy, and Mia leaned forward from her seat next to Sam
and got right in Corey's face and said, "Turn up your ears."

Corey adjusted his transistors and said, "I wasn't listening."

Mia said, "It's impolite not to listen when you're in somebody else's house."

Corey said, "Yes, ma'am. Hello, everyone."

What would Scot make of this sleepy-eyed boy with the jet
black hair and cowboy boots to match? Corey didn't say
much, and he was remarkably passive, or maybe he was
scared stiff around strangers. He kept one hand on Billy's
knee, and he couldn't remember my name or Sam's when
Mia told him to say good-bye. As soon as he was out the
door, Corey turned around and stared blankly at the pink
rosettes Scot had stuck on the frame in September, and then
he turned off his ears, an auditory option that I knew his
brother would envy.

twenty-eight

It snowed several times during the first few weeks of December, and each time I hoped it would melt before I had to shovel, and Scot hoped school would be canceled, and we would sit in the kitchen with our cups and bowls before us, listening as the man on the radio recited the brief list of postponed classes and community services, and then Sam would finish meditating, and Scot would shower, and I would shovel a few inches of slush off the front stairs, and that night we would discuss vacation plans or summer camp or how much money Scot would be allotted for the purchase of Christmas gifts.

Almost every day, Scot visited the bank to ask Art Timilty's advice about the value per penny of a nose-hair clipper for Sam, or a secondhand beret for me, or a raccoon-proof garbage can for Mildred and the Georges. Sam stopped by the bank to thank Art for the consulting services, and in his normal, narcotized voice Art said it was nothing, and Sam said he'd like to take Art to lunch someday, and Art blandly said, "Okey-dokey. Just following Akela."

I said, "He said what?"

Sam said, "I thought he said 'Attila,' but it was 'Akela,'" and he handed me a sticker that Art had handed him. It was a yellow arrow flying through the air with the words, *Follow Akela!* We immediately got out the magnifying glass and looked it up in our dictionaries and encyclopedias, but we were stumped.

I wanted to know if Art had dropped any other clues about Akela, who sounded like an Egyptian god to me, perhaps because Scot and I had recently visited the mummies at the Museum of Fine Arts.

Sam said, "You can ask him yourself."

Art had pressed a few buttons on both of his watches, and said, "The sixteenth appears to be a Saturday, and I could be at your house by five minutes before noon. You and Ed live on Finn Street. Should I bring anything?"

When Scot heard about the lunch date, he worried that Mr. Timilty would expect a Christmas gift, and his limited budget couldn't tolerate any more surprises. "I already have to buy something extra, for Corey," Scot announced, "and I hope you're telling Mia in advance so they won't be embarrassed. They'll have to get something for me. It can just be something affordable, but we should probably remind Billy I don't really use yo-yos. He used to buy me about a yo-yo every month when I was a kid."

He had taken to the idea of having a brother—"Corey's a half," Scot explained to Joey one afternoon in the backyard, "so nobody's forcing us to live in the same state, and we don't even match blood types"—though he was annoyed when Sam and I told him we couldn't be absolutely sure there were no more unidentified relatives out there. He mostly blamed "Julie's drugs" for the confusion, but the fin-

ish on the photograph of Julie that hung in our kitchen was
fading from glossy to matte. When Scot was frustrated by a
house policy that he considered unfair—no colored contact
lenses, no dieting (grapefruit was allowed and encouraged,
but only one a day, and no canned nondairy supplements)—
he blamed Julie for messing up his life and sending him to
Finn Street or, depending on his mood, "this prison," or
"Nowheresville,"or—Scot's   favorite—"double-N   Funn
Street, get it?"

Sam and I were his guardians, and sometimes his wardens,
and Julie was losing her hold on him, and unlike me, Scot
never considered Billy or his household an option. Maybe it
was all those yo-yos. He was happy to think about the three of
us spending Christmas in D.C. with the three of them, and
though he was worried about the airplane ride, when Sam
showed him a brochure for the turreted hotel where we
would be staying, Scot saw a castle full of personal-sized hair
and body creams and sewing kits, and he convinced Mildred
to let him borrow her blinders for the flight. "She says being
blind is scarier than any plane, and I might learn to be grateful for my eyes, which is the spirit of the season."

But for all of our success, Scot still didn't have a sport or a
team, which had risen from the middle to the top of Sam's
list of goals, and thus to the top of Scot's, and thus to the top
of mine. We all agreed that Scot needed physical exercise,
more friends, and something to replace ¡Hola!, which had
degenerated into corn chips and videotapes of American sit-
coms dubbed into Spanish. For a few weeks, we worked on it
together. We formed an assembly line.

I generated ideas and possibilities. For instance: What
about a noncompetitive group activity that doesn't require a
lot of experience?

Sam brought facts to the table. For instance: There is an indoor, co-ed soccer league at the Y on Wednesday and Friday afternoons. No tryouts, no cuts.

Scot presented pertinent conflicts, aversions, or incompetencies. For instance: When we play soccer in gym, mostly we just kick each other in the shins to make bruises, and Mrs. Morita won't let Joey go into the Y because of what happened to that kid who got raped there. Plus I have Super Computing on Wednesdays.

Ed: Something theatrical?

Sam: Saturday-morning group acting and stagecraft classes at the Jewish Community Center.

Scot: Already cast as a reindeer in the school play and probably going to be George Washington for the history class production in February because most kids can't memorize their lines. I know Mr. Koester is Jewish, but are we?

Ed: An indoor-outdoor sport that is also a lifelong activity.

Sam: Roller-blading.

Scot: If you say so, but we better rent, not buy, right, Ed?

Our factory was constantly busy, and we produced absolutely nothing. This gave rise to labor disputes until, one evening, Sam and I remembered we were management. We could demand results. But while we were trying to craft an ultimatum that we could live with, two crises in Scot's life woke him up to the urgency of joining any club, team, or circus that would have him.

The first crisis was half his fault and half mine.

Sam and I and Scot had accepted an invitation for Friday night cards with the Koesters. It was our first reunion since the pies, and Joan wisely chose gin rummy, so there were no teams and Scot could play. Hank fell asleep first, and Scot eventually conked out in a soft chair, and we had a brief flirtation with the cognac at Greg's insistence. Joan claimed he was trying to ply us with drink so we would agree with him about his mother, who was quite alive and hoping to cash in her Thanksgiving mini-strokes ("heartburn and heavy breathing," according to Joan) for a bedroom on Finn Street. It was late when we left, and Scot had asked me to wake him, but I didn't. Sam carried him home.

The next morning, I found Scot sitting in the kitchen with a box and a shovel. Instead of muttering good morning, Scot said, "You've really done it this time, Ed." In the box, a dead kitten was slowly thawing. Carla's pregnant cat had delivered only one kitten out of four that had been expected, and because Carla considered Scot her best best friend, he got it. By arrangement, Carla had dropped it off the night before and left it on the back porch. "It was supposed to be a surprise, like the pie," said Scot. "You broke your promise. You didn't wake me up. Carla is gonna kill me."

He was surprisingly not squeamish about poking and displaying the corpse, which made it hard for me to keep my spirits in the funereal range. I was pleased to know that the doors to medical school were open to him.

As soon as Sam heard the story, he banned all surprise deliveries. Living things, even plants, were not to be imported without prior approval.

I was not guilty for having failed to wake Scot when we carried him home from the Koesters. How could I have known what lay dying at our door? But when I went to the cellar to trade the snow shovel Scot had selected for a burial spade, I saw that Scot had torn down his curtain. There, deep in that hidden corner, he had built a cat palace. He'd repaired a balsa-wood crate, painted it red, and lined it with sterile cotton—the bed. The pillow was a pink makeup sponge. On the ceiling, he'd hung up several ribbons and strings of beads for swatting. Kitty litter in a cookie tin. Two cans of sardines. Cottage-cheese containers for milk, water, and solid food. And a dowel screwed into a low shelf, to which Scot had glued a nubbly strip of carpet, for scratching.

I should've known. He'd been talking about cats.

Sam said, "We can't catch everything."

I nodded.

Sam added, "But when Scot posts a Do Not Enter sign, you're supposed to put on a gas mask and break down the door."

I nodded again.

Scot was in mourning, but he wouldn't attend the burial.

He and Sam meditated for five minutes, and I prayed that I wouldn't accidentally dig up all of Mildred's bulbs.

Carla was livid. She dropped Scot to the fourth and lowest spot on her chart of best friends, and though she continued to stop by for acne advice and coaching on her spread-eagle jumps, Scot was never allowed to forget that he was only one mistake away from the dreaded second-best-friend status.

The next crisis was not something we could bury in the backyard. Scot and his classmates watched Miss Paul and two practice teachers physically subdue and restrain Anton, whose medications finally failed him. It was Anton's last day in the mainstream. He was shot up with something stronger and shipped off to a residential school for disturbed children, and Scot never saw him again.

That night, all through dinner, Scot didn't want to talk about it. He and Sam meditated. The resident atheist made tea.

We were all reading in the living room when Scot said, "Anton is big, but they know how to hurt you. One of the teachers kept his knee on Anton's neck and stuck something in his mouth. Are they allowed to do that to anybody who gets out of line?"

Sam said, "They'll never be allowed to do it to you."

Scot said, "When I squatted down to look in Anton's eyes, Miss Paul said, 'Take your goddamned place,' and she put a couple of us on detention. Anton wouldn't close his eyes. They wanted him to, but he wasn't afraid of them."

Scot was sitting cross-legged on his sofa. We'd made a fire. He was wearing an undershirt, his nightshirt, one of Sam's sweaters, and he was cold.

Sam said, "Anton shouldn't have to suffer just because."

Scot nodded. He knew what Sam meant.

Sam said, "You've been a good friend to Anton."

Scot said, "What am I supposed to say to Miss Paul now?"

I said, "You can certainly can say you are sorry Anton is gone."

Scot said, "But do I say anything about her violence?"

Sam said, "The ball is in her court."

I could see that Scot was confused. I said, "Suppose we wrote a note together? We could ask her to write us a letter explaining what happened. Would that help?"

Scot mulled it over for a few seconds. He nodded. "I get it. The ball's in her court."

Sam said, "And you probably shouldn't tell Miss Paul until after Christmas, but you can tell yourself that you will be at a new school next year."

Scot perked up. "Private?"

Sam said, "Probably private." He looked at me for confirmation.

I said, "Probably private." I could say it was because of Anton, or the TV requirement, or the history curriculum we were told was "designed to emphasize the meaning of the past in modern life," which explained why Scot was writing his own autobiography instead of reading the ones written by Benjamin Franklin or Frederick Douglass. I could say all that. But as I said to Sam that night in bed, I also had to say I was sorry that Scot seemed so eager to splash on the perfume of privilege, l'eau de private school.

Sam said, "The mainstream stinks, too."

The school Sam had picked out was progressive and old— among adolescents, that meant casual sex but no teenage pregnancies. Scot would have to compete for admission with many other able kids, and like any normal Cambridge parent in his position, Sam called his attorney, Barbara, who was the vice-president of the school's board of trustees. She was an alum, too, and though I didn't find that as reassuring as Sam did, I didn't have an attorney. I didn't know anybody who was influential enough to get a cat into obedience school.

twenty-nine

I was seated with my coffee and the newspaper. Sam was stirring his kasha. Scot was standing beside the refrigerator, staring at the calendar. He said, "Do you know what today is? Today is the Friday before the Saturday before the Saturday before Christmas." He looked beset.

We were leaving for D.C. on the Saturday before Christmas. Scot had picked up and priced most of the merchandise in Cambridge, and he had yet to purchase a single present. Sam had pared Scot's list down to three people—Hank Koester, Mildred, and Corey. Sam and I never exchanged Christmas gifts, and Sam had asked Scot to think of something he could do for us on the Saturday before Christmas instead of buying us things. On the morning of our flight, we were going to exchange our true Christmas gifts, as Sam called them.

Scot had two concerns. The first was Nula, but I said Nula was family, and Scot said he would have to think of something to do for her, too. His second concern was more in the spirit of traditional Christmas.

As Scot said, "What about me? Just happy thoughts? No presents?"

Sam smiled and said, "We'll have to see what Santa Claus decides."

Scot said, "Sam."

Sam said, "Scot."

Scot said, "Sam!"

Sam said, "Scot!"

Scot smiled and turned to me. He said, "When you see Santa Claus, Ed, tell him if we're going to Cape Cod in the summer like he said, I might need a snorkel and a mask and fins. Maybe a net for minnows. I also sometimes use a nose plug if there are waves."

He was also getting a bike, not only because neither of us wanted to lend him our cars for his trips to the pharmacy, and not only because Sam and I had bikes and sometimes rode them to the river in the spring and to the flat bay beaches on the Cape, but because in his eleven-odd years among the species famed for inventing the wheel no one had bothered to teach Scot how to ride a bike. Yo-yos.

When I got to the office, Nula was leaning out the window with a cigarette and a telephone. She was wearing red mittens but no hat. Eleanor Covena wasn't there, as usual, but she also wasn't there because she had quit. I'd already spoken to Marco about hiring someone to replace her, and he'd said, "You have my holy vows that Eleanor Covena will never work in Italy again." Two days later, a courier delivered two first-class airplane tickets to Milan, and a note: "Quite easy to get a train from Milan. Go see Giotto's chapel in Padua, and from there it is only 30 miles to Venice, and from Venice you can see everything else. Sylvia."

The tickets were on my desk. Nula had faxed our production schedule for the first quarter of the new year to Milan. She had crossed out every day in the third week of February and labeled it "Presidents' Week/National Holidays." She and Sam were convinced I was taking the trip. But I knew I was not.

I was not going to the Berkshires to paint that maple tree. I was not going to Padua to sit in the Scrovegni Chapel and see everything I had not seen. I was not going to stand on the Grand Canal and think of Scot's nose plugs and reconsider my choices. I would be holding on to Sam's beard and, when need be, borrowing Mildred's blinders.

Nula crushed her cigarette into an espresso cup and, to someone in Milan, she said, "Yes, yes, yes. Sì, sì, sì. You understand, now. All of the electrical workers in Boston. Sì. A big march today. You understand. In the streets. Sì. Communistas. Sì, sì, sì. Ciao. Ciao." She hung up the phone and said, "Don't take your coat off. I just declared a citywide strike. We're at least three issues ahead of Milan, and I'm wearing more layers than Scot, and it's so cold in this joint that I can't tell whether or not I'm smoking."

I opened my handsome new portable computer and said, "I just want to answer a few author queries and check—"

Nula slammed it shut and pulled my plug. "You weren't listening. The communists cut off our power."

I said, "Give me an hour."

Nula said, "I've got Scot's Christmas gift in the car. I can't drop it off over the weekend while he's there, and starting next Monday I've got myself lined up with five dates in six days, so I won't be making any deliveries before you leave for D.C."

"Five blind dates?"

Nula nodded. "I called up everyone who typically sends me a houseplant to kill or gift certificates to take myself to the movies, and I asked for dates instead."

"Dinner dates?"

"Of course," Nula said. "This way, when they don't work out, at least I've been on a crash diet. Now, let's go get Scot's gift."

There were two beautifully wrapped and ribboned boxes in the backseat of her car. We climbed in, and then Nula rested her forehead on the steering wheel, as if maybe she needed a nap.

I said, "Want me to drive?"

She said, "I'm just trying to figure out which one of us is Billy and which one is Sam."

We idled until the heat kicked in. Without warning, Nula peeled out of the parking space and didn't stop until we were in Lenox. She handed me the two beautiful boxes—a new set of pastel pencils and a pad.

Nula napped.

I drew.

We drove back to Boston and returned to our respective homes, like a couple of brothers.

thirty

Early in the morning of the Saturday before the Saturday before Christmas, we gathered for a strategy meeting after breakfast. We sat on our sofas. Scot brought the yellow pages. He was compiling a list of stores he wanted to visit with Sam, who was confirming our reservations in D.C. I was assigned the task of meeting with Mildred, who had left a message announcing that she had "urgent news about the Burlington situation; P.S., the boys are coming back."

When he heard it, Scot said, "If Anton was still around, he'd crack open Tony's bald head."

He was scared.

I'd left my list of things to do in the bedroom, and Scot kindly offered to retrieve it, and when he brought it back, he said, "I wasn't invading anything, but I noticed a sticker on the desk. With an arrow. It was under the list," which he handed to me.

"You can have that sticker," I said.

He looked suspicious. "Where'd you get it?"

I said, "Mr. Timilty gave it to Sam."

Scot said, "Oh. It's Sam's."

I said, "You can really have it."

Scot said, "Okay," and wandered back to his sofa. "When Sam gets off the phone, can I call Joey Morita and tell him about private school and stuff before we have to leave for Washington? He knows how to keep a secret. He has his own private counselor."

"You're going to see him all next week in school."

Scot said, "Maybe just a quick hello, then."

And then Sam made a quick call to Jeremy, who was sick, and suddenly Scot was on his was to Joey's, and I was on my way to Mildred's, and Sam was going to the office to cover for his partner, and I reminded all of us about twenty times to be home for lunch with Art Timilty.

Mildred was in a bad mood, not because of what she'd heard, but because of what she hadn't heard. Her principal method of acquiring information about the Burlingtons was not sophisticated. She made George Junior stand in the street or wander around in Louisa Bamford's yard and report back on what he heard. The moving men had removed most of Andrea's furniture and then delivered new, unupholstered wood and chrome things, "expensive modern stuff that apparently doesn't get up her nose," said Mildred. The rest was speculation. George Junior had seen Ryan and Tony eating dinner with Andrea and their mean second father on Thursday evening, and George Junior was fairly certain the boys had arrived with suitcases and left without them, but George Junior had gone inside for a few minutes to get a beer, and he had to admit to Mildred that he might have missed something.

Spring really couldn't come fast enough for Mildred. She didn't like the cold, and she hated to rely on George Junior's amateur snooping. Had the weather been fair, Mildred would have been haranguing me with the number of chops each Burlington boy had eaten.

I said, "Louisa Bamford ought to sell her house as is."

Mildred said, "She did. Didn't I tell you? I knew that a week ago. Oh, that's the real news, Eddy." Mildred was back in bloom. "Louisa sold her house to Andrea Burlington's allergy doctor from Harvard. He got it for a song. He never even told Andrea he'd put in a bid. He used her fake allergies to jack down the price, that's all. Mark my words, before the snow's melted, he'll be out painting those shingles with the best chemicals money can buy. Andrea will need more than a mask. That's why Andrea's bringing her boys back. She wants revenge on the doctor who betrayed her."

A few hours later, Sam and I stared out from our living room window and wondered if we'd like the new neighborhood doctor. Scot had called and begged for permission to eat lunch with Joey, and it was granted. And Art Timilty walked right down the middle of Finn Street in khaki pants, an olive green sweater, and a cloth khaki cap. As he neared our house, we noticed his red-and-green neckerchief.

And I thought, Scot is going to be sorry he missed this.

We sat on the sofas. There was a platter of sandwiches and sparkling water.

Sam said, "Any trouble finding us?"

Art said, "The Cub Scout follows Akela—"

Sam said, "The sticker."

Art said, "There's more. It's the Law of the Pack. The Cub Scout follows Akela. The Cub Scout helps the pack go. The pack helps the Cub Scout grow. The Cub Scout gives good-will."

It just got worse. Art had "taken the liberty" of bringing along a blue-and-gold neckerchief for Scot, diagrams of the Cub Scout hierarchy—from Tigers, Bobcats, Wolves, and Bears (Really—Bears) to Webelos (that was secret code language: We'll be loyal scouts). He showed us a picture of his pack—five skinny Scot-like boys dressed in blue-and-gold beanies and shorts and sashes, which were plastered with activity badges testifying to their expertise in art, reading, swimming, jumping, history, camping, first aid, and absolutely every skill and talent we hoped Scot might acquire.

We had discovered Scot's lost tribe.

Art had more. He had stickers and colorful brochures for summer camp and ceremonial oaths and secret handshakes and pledges to family and God and country and neatness and a whole new and more complicated world of Boy Scouting as soon as Scot hit sixth grade or earned the Arrow of Light, which involved a series of tests that proved you had acquired the virtues of Akela, a brave Brave, who had made his fame hunting, and gaining wisdom as well as some meat, pelts, and humility.

Art said, "I'm an Eagle Scout myself, and on one of Scot's visits to the bank it occurred to me that he might take to scouting. He could jump right in as a Webelo."

Even before Art said it, everyone who'd ever seen Scot instinctively knew he was a Webelo.

Sam judiciously said, "It's an interesting idea, Art."

Art adjusted his neckerchief.

Sam looked a little sad when he said, "Of course, Ed and I are gay."

Art said, "Gotcha. Gotcha. Supreme Court?"

Sam nodded. The Boy Scouts of America had won a ruling from the Court upholding the organization's right to
banish gay scoutmasters.

Art said, "I understand. Of course, I'm not recruiting you
and Ed. Our den already has a leader. Me. Scouting is for
kids, and this is Cambridge, after all, after all. We don't deal
with sex in Scouting, of course. Scot would be safe with
me."

Sam smiled.

"Scot's always been safe with you, Art. And I think it's
safe to say that Scot's only question will be when he can
start wearing the hat. We'll need to talk about it some more
first, though."

Art said, "Ask away, ask . . . Oh. You and Ed. Natch. I hope
I haven't overstepped."

Sam said, "No. Ed and I are overwhelmed, I think. We just
need some time to read a little more about Webelos."

Art said, "Catching on quickly, Sam. Kids love the lingo."

There were four uneaten sandwiches, and because I had
no idea what to say, I asked Art if he would take them home,
and he did. Courteous? Thrifty? Obedient?

Sam and I wasted the next two hours of a sunny Saturday
telling each other what we both already knew. The Boy
Scouts did not disapprove of boys like Scot. They disap-
proved of boys like us. And Scot needed more than we could
give him. We were the adults. We didn't have to wear our
hearts on our sleeves if it meant Scot wouldn't get a chance
to wear a neckerchief.

I said, "The unnerving thing is not whether or not to let
him do it. We're going to let him do it. Right?"

Sam said, "I have to make some tea."

I followed him. "What scares me is that you and I basically spent the last two weeks with Scot trying to invent the Cub Scouts. Everything we said is right out of the manual."

Sam filled the kettle and selected a mild herb tea. "I knew I would be less and less useful to Scot as he got older," Sam said, and then he stroked his beard and smiled. "But I really wasn't prepared to feel like a liability."

And then for another hour, I walked up and down the stairs reciting the names of gay Catholic friends, and famous civil-rights activists, and Lord Baden-Powell, trying to figure out where Scot and Sam and I fit into the litany, and Sam sat in the bedroom and stared at the dead end, maybe meditating, maybe wishing we could rewrite the Supreme Court ruling or amend the manual a bit. Greg Koester came by with Hank and a three-foot Christmas tree in a pot of dirt, "just in case you guys have changed your minds and want the smell around the house before you go to D.C. And to remind you that Joan is going to teach us how to play bridge—and how to get along—on New Year's Eve." Greg spotted the neckerchief and the brochures, and he didn't ask.

On one of my many passes by the bedroom, I heard Sam humming or chanting, which was a new twist, and I called Nula. She said we were blowing the whole thing out of proportion. Come September, she said, Scot would ditch the beanie.

"Have you ever walked by that new school of his? You don't see a lot of Eagle Scouts out raking the lawns." Nula had been tossed out of most of the better day schools in Cambridge, so I trusted her. "By the fall, you'll be wondering about his credit-card limit, and was that permission slip you signed for a field trip or an acid trip?"

I said, "Thanks. But for now—"

"Sure. God and country for now," Nula said. "And if he doesn't cut it as a Cub Scout, there's probably an opening or two in the Nazi Youth League."

I ran upstairs and told Sam we ought to delay the decision until after Corey and Christmas and maybe until after college, too.

Sam said, "Let's at least give ourselves a week. Or right after New Year's Eve, when we're all tired and calm."

Optimistically, I added, "We'll tell Scot exactly how we feel, and we'll all come to a decision that fits."

We hugged. We sat on the edge of the bed and congratulated ourselves. We were getting better at this. We were learning to be receptive but deliberate. We could not control the future, but we could take time into our own hands, and it was already easier to imagine how we could help Scot make a mindful choice, because we didn't know that Scot and Joey had come in through the back door and sat down together on a sofa with the pile of pamphlets between them.

When we joined them, they were arguing about something Scot had written in a notebook, but they shushed each other and settled down quickly. We exchanged pleasantries, and Scot twice referred to Art Timilty as "The Amphibian," which was then outlawed, and finally Sam said, "Have you ever heard of the Cub Scouts, boys?"

Joey said, "Not until today I don't think. Maybe in passing."

Scot said, "You know I have. He told you, right?"

Sam said, "Who?"

Scot said, "Your lunch guest." His voice was wavering between scared and surly.

I said, "Don't use that tone of voice." Or maybe my father said that.

"Sorry," Scot said. "Just nerves."

Joey kicked Scot in the shin and said, "I told you. They don't even know."

Scot said, "Oh, good going, Joey. Or should I say, Thanks, Mr. Beans? Thanks for the big spill."

Joey looked at his sneakers.

Sam didn't say a word, and neither did I.

"If you want," Scot said, still glaring at Joey, "really, really want me to try the Cub Scouts again, okay. But we called Joey's counselor and made up another plan if you want to hear it."

Joey said, "Two. Two ideas."

Scot swatted him with his notebook.

Sam and I didn't look at each other. I don't know exactly what Sam was thinking, but I was praying again.

Scot said, "I thought Mr. Timilty came by to tell you about me getting kicked out of Cub Scouts back in Baltimore."

Joey said, "He kept flunking neatness."

Scot said, "I could've stayed even after flunking neatness and a few other things, I think, on account of I was only like a bobcat or something. Maybe a wolf."

Joey said, "Yeah, a wolf is what you said at my house."

"Yeah, probably a wolf," said Scot. "Then a couple of older kids put a lot of pressure on me to bring hair spray to the den mother's house one day. They had the matches, but I got blamed for setting her kitchen table on fire, even though it was just the paper napkins and the tablecloth." Scot shrugged. "Maybe some certificates." He nodded. "Somebody said a curtain, but I never saw that."

Sam started to shake, and he walked right out of the living room and into the kitchen. He called back, "I thought the kettle was on," but I could see that he had his hands braced against the counter, trying to control his laughter.

I had to go help Sam make tea.

Before we returned to the living room, I said, "No more manuals. Right? He can camp out with Joey on Mildred's patio."

Sam smiled. He said, "You know who needs neckerchiefs? The Supreme Court."

Scot and Joey were all business when we returned. With telephone advice from Joey's counselor, and Liz Morita's seal of approval, they had come up with a plan.

Joey said, "You guys probably remember I told you, I'm part Japanese."

We nodded.

"So Scot and me think we should try karate," he said, then he poked Scot.

"It's ancient art and self-defense." Scot was reading from his notes. "And discipline." He looked up to see how it was going. He said, "There are also the robes."

"And belts," said Joey. "Belts is about the most important part not to leave out, Scot."

Scot raised his eyebrows. "I never would have remembered."

Joey said, "My mother said to tell you there's a karate place in walking distance. To both schools. Scot told about private school."

Scot said, "Ed gave me permission."

Sam raised his cup of tea in the air and said, "I think this is a very good plan. I am very impressed by your initiative. Both of you."

We all sipped our weak tea.

Joey said, "Say the other part."

Scot said, "We came up with something else when we were walking over here. Just Joey and me. No adults."

I said, "Another activity?"

Joey said, "We weren't sure if you take lessons or learn it on your own. And we're not completely sure it's for boys."

Scot shrugged, "We can just say it or just not say it. It's up to you."

Sam and I both leaned way back in our sofas.

Scot said, "It's just for a little fun, maybe." He looked at Joey's sneakers. "We've never even tried it." He looked at the ceiling. "Unless maybe a couple of times with sticks."

Joey said, "Yeah. We tried it with sticks."

Scot nodded. "You know, twirling. Baton."

thirty-one

On the Saturday before Christmas, Sam and I woke to the worst odor ever. It was almost seven o'clock. We were exhausted and already behind schedule. We put on our bathrobes.

Scot was standing on the front porch in his nightshirt and poncho and heavy red socks. The door was open.

"Merry Christmas. You just missed Nula."

Sam said, "What are you doing?"

Scot said, "I'm done."

I asked about the smell. It was nail-polish remover. And it works on stickers.

Scot's gift. The pink roses were gone.

Scot screeched, "Sam!"

I instinctively grabbed Sam's arm.

Scot said, "You're so handsome!"

Sam's gift. The beard was gone.

Sam and Scot both looked at me for a reaction. I said, "Aren't we going to meditate?"

My gift? The resistance was gone.

We sat together in the spare room with our eyes half-closed, and then we ate croissants from the Heyday courtesy of Nula, who had also stuck a single gold cardboard star on the top of our bare tree. There was a message taped to it, but the print was tiny. Scot zipped upstairs and returned with the dictionary, and he pulled out the magnifying glass.

Sam handed the star to Scot. He said, "Your name is printed on the back. It's for you."

Scot put the star on the table and sat on his sofa. He leaned forward and read, and then he slumped back against his cushions. Very slowly, Scot said, "It's a real star. Named it after me. It's official. U.S. Government. And there's something else I haven't even read yet." He leaned forward again, and read aloud, very, very, very slowly. "You are the finest light in the Cambridge sky. Shine forever on my bright Finn Street."

We were golden.

We were high above a spread of cotton clouds. Sam was staring out the airplane window. I was eating a croissant I'd snagged before we left the house. Scot lifted his blinders. He looked vaguely in the direction of the window. He shrugged. He shoved the blinders back on his head. He said, "Will the gift shop be open in the hotel when we get there?"

Sam said, "Yes."

Scot said, "I think I left Corey's present."

I said nothing.

Scot said, "It was in my poncho."

Sam said nothing.

"In the Men's Room in the airport, probably," Scot said. "Maybe with my mittens." He opened the lid of the built-in ashtray. "And a couple of dollars." He drew down his shades. He pressed a button and pushed back on his seat. When he was fully reclined, he said "Ed?"

I said, "Yes?"

Scot said, "Was I wearing my hat?"